The Metamorphosis of Longing
Tales of libido, albedo, sex, and suspense

By Malcolm Brautigan

Edited by Jonathan P. Thompson

***

BURNING SUNFLOWER
Publishing

First Burning Sunflower Publishing Edition, July 2019

Published by Jonathan P. Thompson and Burning Sunflower Publishing

www.jonathanpthompson.com

ISBN: 978-0-578-54276-8

Cover art and design by Jonathan P. Thompson

For Wendy, of course.

Editor's Introduction

This odd assortment of stories — perhaps we could call it a fractured narrative — arrived in the inbox of Burning Sunflower's erotica imprint, Carpe Coitus Press, in February 2020. Carpe Coitus's acquisitions editor, Gwendolyn Topaz, rejected them outright, however, because they did not meet her desired sex-scene-to-word-count ratio. But when she saw the name, Malcolm Brautigan, on the cover letter, she forwarded the stories on to me for my consideration, because Brautigan is a sort of acquaintance of mine, and I am intimately familiar with the minute details of both his public and private life.

As I read, I was surprised to find not a set of unrelated short stories, but a sort of novella that followed a single narrative path, albeit a tangled and warped one with a fractured internal logic, that was interspersed with seemingly unrelated short stories that have the same jarring effect as a pharmaceutical advertisement during a documentary on the opioid crisis, or that Dead Kennedy's song you "cleverly" scrunched between love ballads on the one and only mixtape you made for your high school girlfriend.

Any other editor would have tossed this hot mess straight into the digital dumpster. But two factors kept me from doing so. First, I was able to ascertain that Brautigan had sent these from Silverton, a small mountain town in Colorado. As careful readers probably already know, this is impossible, since the hamlet has been shut off from the outside world by avalanches since late on the night of December 31,

2019, thanks to snowfall levels that have far exceeded all previous records. The phone lines are down, the roads are closed, radio relay towers have been knocked out, and satellite phones rendered largely ineffective due to electromagnetic interference. That means that Brautigan must have gone to extraordinary lengths to acquire a satellite signal to get the stories to us. It seems inconceivable that someone, even Brautigan, would do so in order to submit a collection of fictional smut to a tiny publisher which pays its advances in the form of City Market coupons.

Second, I believe that these stories are not fictional. As I said before, I know Brautigan well, and the narrative part of the story adheres faithfully to the details of Brautigan's life (aside from the sexual prowess his character displays). That leads me to believe that everything that is portrayed here actually occurred, and that this is a warning to the world; the sex stories were added in order to evade detection of those who may be monitoring any signals coming out of Silverton. Because of this we have presented the stories mostly as we received them, with exceptions: Ms. Topaz amped up the sex scenes; and we removed all but two of the extraneous stories, and put those that remained in their own section, so as not to interrupt the flow of the narrative. We left Brautigan's warped chronology intact, along with the cliffhanger at the end of the novella (Part I). We are currently organizing a mission to get into Silverton and recover the rest of the story.

We leave it up to you, dear reader, to decide whether this is just another cli-fi thriller with a heavy dose of sex, or an urgent cry for help. And it is up to you to choose: Either heed the warning and act now, or submit to the smut and let your arousal run wild.

Sincerely,
Jonathan P. Thompson, editor
February 2020

PART ONE

Metamorphosis of Longing
A NOVELLA

1

February 2020

Melissa couldn't help but laugh out loud as she read the want-ad, sandwiched between a phone sex ad and one selling quartz crystal dildos, that appeared about halfway down the third column of the back page of the *Santa Fe Weekly*: "Help wanted in a greenhouse where scents delicious and mighty stream forth, their fragrance so sweet, all things enlivening around."

"Damn," she said, also aloud, oblivious to the sideways glances from her fellow coffee drinkers. "I gotta apply for that one." Not only was the ad's verbiage over the top, but the thought of working in a warm, moist greenhouse at this time of year — when the sky was terminally frog-belly gray, the snow just wouldn't stop, and it was colder than a Silverton-snow-shoveler's ass outside — made her inner thighs quiver with delight.

Besides, law firms and non-profits weren't taking anyone new on, particularly someone with the baggage with which her now-ex husband Malcolm had saddled her. Bartending in the winter just didn't cut it, financially speaking. And there was no fucking way she was going to model for anymore Santa Fe "artists," who were invariably lecherous, late-middle-aged, "enlightened" men with about as much talent as her big toenail.

She allowed herself to imagine herself getting the job, to nurture plants and flowers rather than barflies' alcoholism. She'd finally have

4

a real answer for the assholes at yuppie parties who asked: "So, what do you do?" She'd smoothly reply: "I work in botany. You?" She practiced saying it a few times to her empty coffee cup, drawing out the first syllable, landing hard on the "t," like the British do when they say "butter," so that in the end she sounded like a sheep calling for Tony — "Baaaah-Tonee."

Not that she'd get the job. Her sole experience in botany or plants or gardening or whatnot consisted of a summer in high school working at the local nursery, and she had murdered countless spider plants and even cacti during the course of her life. Still, she had to try. After all, with a want-ad like that, why not? And get this: The floraphile made you apply not by email, not online, not by phone, but by mail. "Write me a letter explaining why you would like to work with my flowers," the ad said. "Send it by post, only, please."

She hopped up and rushed to the counter. "Hey," she said to a barista, whose butt looked pretty scrumptious in those jeans. "Can I borrow a piece of paper? And a pen? And an envelope?"

The guy turned around. Then she recognized him. "Oh. Hey. It's you," she said, "from, ahh, sheeit."
***

From that night at the bar where Melissa worked, that is. His name was Alan. Several months ago he had started coming in, sitting at the bar, ordering one glass of wine, reading, and writing in his notebook. He didn't say much, and Melissa didn't prod him. After three or four times, she asked her colleagues if he came in on nights when she wasn't around. He did not. Alan, apparently, had a thing for Melissa, though he wasn't too good at showing it. On a warm early autumn night, when the smell of piñon smoke and roasting green chiles wafted through the air, he came in, ordered red wine, and sat at the bar reading a Marguerite Duras book, *The Malady of Death*.

That had turned her on. Okay, maybe it wasn't *just* that. She was ovulating, too, and that day's Nia class — which always got her juices flowing — had been especially invigorating, as it was led by both Katie and Evette, and halfway through the session the instructors had chosen to make it nude-Nia, and holy shit those ladies were hot. She followed that up with six espressos, smoked a cigarette during her shift break, and then did a shot of tequila. She hadn't been laid in who-knows-how-long. That's just a figure of speech. She knows exactly how long: fifty-one days, since the weekend her ex-husband Malcolm had showed up unannounced to try to woo her back. As if. She may have had some regrets about what she had done, but there was no way she would fall into the Malcolm thing again. Still, she was happy to allow him to make his best arguments with hands, lips, tongue, and sex before tossing him out the door. He would have had better luck had he just express mailed her a box of those chocolate chip cookies of his.

All of that — nude-Nia, caffeine, nicotine, alcohol, sexual austerity — had gotten stirred together within her and circulated through her blood stream so that her flesh felt as if it were supercharged with static electricity, and anything that touched her, even the brushing of her shirt against her unrestrained breasts, sent a jolting current through her.

Alan, meanwhile, sat passively and indifferently, frustratingly so. He asked questions about her and not-so-surreptitiously wrote the answers down in a reporter's pad. This was a little creepy, sure, but also flattering in an odd way. She intentionally bent over the sink right in front of him, giving him an unmitigated view of her cleavage — he didn't even look. So she gave him another red wine on the house, then another. That seemed to loosen him up a bit. And when she asked him to read a passage from the book to her, he demurred but then relented. His reading voice was nice. The passage he read was melancholy, but also erotic.

When it came time to close she told him he could stay, if he wanted, while she wiped down the bar, stacked the chairs, and so on. He didn't move, and sat and wrote furiously in his notebook, while Melissa worked and strategized her next moves, the bar's standard music mix blaring from the speakers. She was truly at a loss: This guy was either terribly shy, genuinely not interested in Melissa, or, worse yet, interested in her in all the wrong ways. On that particular night Melissa did not have the patience to cultivate any sort of relationship that lasted longer than thirty, sweaty, fist-clenching, back-arching, moan-inducing minutes. How the hell was she going to get this guy to bend her over the bar before the night was done?

The answer came in the form of Frank. Frank Sinatra, that is, whose silky — and bigoted and mobbed-up — voice oozed out of the speakers. And just when ol' Blue Eyes belted out, "I've got you … deep in the heart of me," Alan jumped up from his stool, trotted around the bar, took Melissa in his arms, and began dancing her around the place. He wasn't the most refined dancer, but that was a good thing, and the way he took the lead, guiding her with gentle pressure to the small of her back or the palm of her hand, showed that he had potential after all. As the song came to a close, he gave her one last twirl, dipped her in such a way that his thigh was in between hers, pressing up against her sex, and looked her deeply in the eyes. Then the song ended, replaced by something by Bono — instant buzzkill — and Alan turned his eyes down and sheepishly started back for his barstool and notebook.

"No," she said, grabbing his hand as if to lead him on another dance, and dragged him around the bar and into the back room. She shut off the music, pushed him up against the wall, pulled off his shirt, and then her own, pressing her hardened nipples against his smooth chest, and kissed him hard on the mouth. Alan clearly was not prepared for this, clearly had not come to the bar expecting or even hoping for anything remotely like this to occur. He wore an expression not unlike a deer blinded by headlights, just before it gets pummeled by a big rig, otherwise known as Melissa Nyquist's supercharged libido.

That did not stop Melissa. Indeed, the poor guy's reticence inflamed her all the more. She unbuttoned his pants while still devouring his mouth. With an agile leg-foot motion of a dancer or a yogi, she pushed his trousers down around his ankles, and removed what was left of her own clothing, including underwear that had gone past the stage of mere dampness. Finally she stopped kissing him, stepped back a little to get a look at his body, and pushed down his tight boxer briefs. If Alan had seemed a bit reluctant, his sex made up for it, leaping free like an engorged jack-in-the-box. She put both hands on his shoulders and forced him down so that he was sitting on the floor, his back up against the wall, and she mounted him and began grinding away, one thrust, two… something was wrong. She stopped and opened her eyes. Alan had a look of pleading on his face, his arms flailed outward like a chicken flapping its wings, and he let out a juicy cry from the back of his throat. She felt the warmth spread inside of her.

"You didn't come already, did you?" Melissa asked, her tone both desperate and harsh. "Ohhhhh… damnit!"

"Sorry. I'm sorry. It's just that I … you feel so damned good."

To his credit, the guy had gone down on her with great enthusiasm after a little respite, and she had gone home that night feeling sated if still a little let down. It was like when you are dead set on wolfing down a greasy burger and a milkshake, and you show up at Blake's Lotaburger and it is closed and you end up eating a banh mi from the cart next door, which is tastier, healthier, and better all around, but still just doesn't quite work. After all, she hadn't dragged him into the back room for a lingual love affair, she had done so to fuck him until her eyeballs popped out of her head with pleasure. Men these days.

As if the coitus brevis weren't dismaying enough, he sent the first text precisely one hour after they had parted. "I had a great time. <Heart emoji>." The second one arrived at six the next morning. And by noon, and text number twelve, Alan was clearly growing desperate due to her lack of response. She ignored his messages for another forty-eight hours or so, at which point she got horny again and decided Alan was better than nothing. She invited him over, this time making him wear one of those desensitizing condoms, which did the trick.

Before long Alan was kind of hanging around a lot. Too much, in fact. And he was still incessantly jotting crap down in that stupid notebook of his, which he never seemed to let go of. Initially she had thought that he was a writer, and that he was going to model a character after her. Whatever. She had been with enough writers and artists — had served as a "muse" so many times — that this sort of silliness no longer bothered her. But this was something different. Almost sinister. So one day, while he sat on the floor writing more notes, she literally jumped on him, pinned the notebook under her knee, took off his pants, pulled out his penis, and started sucking it with such ardor and skill that Alan didn't know what was happening, allowing her to read the latest notes he had taken: The precise contents of her medicine cabinet, along with random numbers and symbols that looked like code. Creepy.

Nonetheless, she brought him to orgasm. After he shot his wad all over his favorite t-shirt, she promptly sent him and his notebook on his way. For good. He sent her a string of desperate texts and emails and stalked her on social media. She ignored it until, finally, it stopped. A mutual friend had told her that he'd gone off to Virginia, or Macedonia, or somewhere, to work for the CIA or something. But that must have been wrong, because here he was, staring at her across the counter of Santa Fe's most hipper-than-thou coffee dispensary.

"Yeah, me." His face had a greenish tint to it, mixed with a little bit of red. He was blushing. Or he was really, really angry.

"Look, I'm sorry I ghosted you after that," she said, somewhat plaintively. "It's just that I never got all your obsessive, kind of creepy texts. So if I didn't get them I couldn't respond, see?"

"That doesn't make sense."

"Whatever. Look, can I please borrow a piece of paper? And a pen? And an envelope?"

"Envelope?"

"Never mind that. Just the pen and paper. Please?"

"It's a coffee shop, not an office supply store."

"I already spent five… no, seven bucks on a goddamned cup of coffee just because it's single origin or some such bullshit. I don't give a fuck if your coffee's from Farmington. Just tear a sheet out of that damned notebook of yours and give it to me."

With a huff he went back by the espresso machine and rifled through a cabinet, gathering the requested supplies. With his back toward Melissa, he paused, appearing to be writing something down. Probably his phone number. As if. Then he came back with the paper, the pen, and an envelope, complete with a stamp with a drawing of a flower on it. It wasn't until Melissa was putting the envelope in the box that she noticed the digits written in faint pencil on its lower left hand corner. She rolled her eyes and tossed the envelope into the slot.

***

Melissa still didn't have a firm hold on how she had ended up here, eagerly checking her mail in hopes of getting a part-time greenhouse job. Just a few years earlier she had been working as a lawyer at an immigrants' rights organization in Tucson and was several years into a happy if stagnant marriage with Malcolm Brautigan, an environmental reporter at the *Tucson Tribune*. Then one day something shifted. It was as if she were a camera, and someone had replaced the filter of maudlin contentment with one of restless ennui.

It was as she staggered about in this malaise that she met Chad: Talkative, vivacious, successful, ambitious, good looking — pretty much everything that Malcolm was not. It was just a friendship, at first, and she had been good with that. Then something happened with Malcolm, maybe he even fucked someone else, as unlikely as that may be. Soon afterward she and Malcolm had gone to Mexico for a week and she found herself missing Chad like crazy the whole time. Within hours after getting home she had concocted some flimsy excuse for going out, went to Chad's place, and screwed him until his eyeballs rolled back into his head. Twice.

Malcolm found out, the marriage fell apart, and she got engaged to Chad. Then, via a convoluted series of events that can be explained at another time, it all fell apart: She lost her job, Malcolm lost his, Chad dumped her, and she had to get the hell out of Tucson. Out of the blue, Malcolm's former editor Laurel had called her up to let her know that her cousin needed a long-term housesitter in Santa Fe. Melissa jumped at it, despite her suspicions about Laurel's motives. She now knew it was a mistake. The economy was shit, the weather was shit, and the people were all out of their gourds with faux spirituality.

Since Melissa moved around a lot she got her mail at a box in a little hole in the wall down on Cerillos road. It had long been obvious that she was the only legitimate box holder in the place — if you could call her legitimate. Everyone else was shipping bomb parts, body parts, or drugs. Her lack of a real address was yet another mark against her when it came to getting the job.

Nonetheless, when she opened the little cubbyhole door during her weekly mail check she found the envelope tucked in with the latest *New Yorker* and something from OmnySyde Collection Agency. She put the latter in the trash where it belonged, tucked the magazine under her arm, and carefully opened the envelope. It felt like she was traveling backwards in time to a simpler and even more sensuous age, when information and words took up physical space and were tangible. The letter was handwritten on thick paper, the kind with texture, the kind that the pen sinks into just a bit, to give each letter a barely perceptible relief. The handwriting was small but beautiful, in perfect cursive. Even the word, "cursive," seemed anachronistic, evoking computer cursors and expletives.

"Dearest Melissa," the flowing script read, "I am delighted that you discovered my advertisement and that it piqued your interest. I should like to meet you in person, if that is agreeable with you. Please come to the address in the ad at three o'clock in the afternoon on Friday, the second of February. Don't be tardy." It was signed: Augustus S. Lavender. What a name. Melissa pictured a waspish old man, tall and dapper and hunched over, with pale, papery skin. He drank tea, had tufts of white, stringy hair sprouting from his ears, and was definitely a pervert. On the upside, as soon as his frail hands found their way to Melissa's breast, thigh, knee, ass, or shoulder, as they surely would, and Melissa took defensive action, his bones would snap and crackle in a decidedly satisfactory way.

She looked at her watch. She could make it if she drove like a New Mexican.

Melissa pulled up to the curb in front of the low, adobe house in her favorite neighborhood just as her heater was starting to blow warm instead of chilly air. She shut off the ignition, stepped out into air so frigid it was on the verge of passing from a gas straight to a solid. Needles of cold shot into her nostrils, her eyeballs iced up, her thin jeans felt like liquid nitrogen against her thighs. The heavy gate leading through the thick, mud-plastered wall opened with a screech. Melissa stopped, waited to see if Augustus had heard and would come out to greet her, saving her from having to knock on the front door. Of course he hadn't. The old goat probably couldn't hear a damned thing. She walked up to the porch, knocked on the wooden door. It was thick. Solid. It hurt her knuckles. Nothing.

She stepped off of the porch. The tip of her nose was frozen now. She was certain that the flesh there was black and would fall off shortly, which, it seemed, could be a bad start to her job interview. She peered around the house and saw a glass wall. Tentatively she walked toward it, the greenhouse coming into view as dry, frosty grass crunched beneath her feet. The glass was steamed up enough to make it almost opaque. All she could see within was green, splashed with amorphous blobs of red, yellow, orange, purple. She tapped gently on the glass, waited precisely three seconds, then turned the brass handle. The door swung open easily, and she quickly closed it behind her to keep the heat inside.

Oh and what a heat it was. Warm. Wet. Fragrant. Sultry. The rich profusion of flowers confounded her. Melissa was struck by the urge to undress and let the miniature jungle ravage her, let the giant, prurient flowers straddle her, penetrate her with their pollen-dusted pistils. She closed her eyes, opened her mouth, tilted her head back, and ...

"You must be Melissa." The voice was soft, deep, smooth, and certainly didn't sound like it came from a feeble old man. She opened her eyes to find that she was looking directly into those of Augustus S. Lavender: Green like the murk of a river in summer, speckled with gold, intense but gentle, too. A warm stirring crept from her upper thighs into her belly. For a long moment, she couldn't speak.

"It's okay," he said, smiling. "The flowers tend to leave people speechless."

"Yes," Melissa stammered. "The flowers."

"Your job, if you choose to accept it, will be to take care of them. The flowers, I mean. While I'm away."

"Where are you going?"

"I travel often to procure new plants or to botany conferences, that sort of thing. It's important that I have the right person for the job. I've interviewed a dozen people already. None of them has worked out yet."

"You mean I would be alone?"

"Just you and the flowers, yes."

"Oh. You see, I didn't realize that. I'm afraid that I ... well, I'm not really a gardener, it's just that I thought ..."

"You thought?"

"I thought ... Wait. I know where it came from: Goethe. Goethe!"

"Yes?"

"Your ad in the Weekly! You got it from Goethe. That poem about flowers."

He smiled. His teeth were charmingly crooked. "Yes. *The Metamorphosis of Plants*. Not only lovely verse, but also scientifically accurate. You've read it?"

"Yeah, in college, for biology class, if you can believe it."

"I can, indeed." He looked at her, sizing her up. "You're hired if you'd still like the job."

"No, no, I don't. I'm not… I don't know much about plants."

"Ah, but you do! You've read Goethe. Besides, the idea of a green thumb is a myth," he said. "What matters is being able to understand each plant's needs and desires. And you seem to possess that ability. Please accept the job. I will train you before my first trip."

Again, warmth flooded her thighs, and, without even asking what the job paid, she accepted.

Her first days at work were grueling. She followed Augustus around and took notes as he laid out, in detail, the family tree of each flower, fruit, and shrub, fluidly reciting each barbarous-sounding name. He humbly pointed out rare orchids such as the *Cyprepedium rothschildianum*. It wasn't in bloom, and looked pretty spindly to her, but August's eyes grew wide as he described its flower's plum-colored stripes and hairy petals. "I do, do hope you will stick around long enough to see it."

The tomato vine was so tall, so bushy, that she thought at first that it was some sort of tree. Then she saw the yellow fruit bending down the branches, and she smelled that tomato-vine smell, a smell that can only be described as deep-green, on par with the smell of a hay-field in June, just after the first cutting. The tomatoes, themselves, brought back a memory of a time in San Francisco, on a work trip, when she was sitting in a restaurant with an open kitchen, and watching the bruschetta girl work. The young woman apparently had one and only one job: toast the bread to a crispy, golden color; drizzle it with olive oil; smear it with a big clove of garlic; and then take an ultra-ripe tomato and crush it in her hand and onto the toasted bread. Melissa had been mesmerized by the moment of the tomato crush. Forget the nerve-numbing pounding of pornography, *this* was sexy. Melissa sat there for hours, sipping wine and, when it seemed like bruschetta girl would get a break, she ordered more bruschetta just so she could see it all again. She will forever rue not asking the young woman to go home with her, but consoles herself with the knowledge that the reality wouldn't have lived up to the fantasy, that the bruschetta girl wasn't old and wise enough to do her like she did that tomato. No, her real regret was that she hadn't applied for the position of bruschetta girl, herself.

A fig tree with big, brown fruit weighing heavily on the weirdly bare branches beckoned. Melissa reflexively reached for one of the fruit, but August, as he preferred to be called, ("but please not Gus or Augie,"), firmly took hold of her wrist to stop her. "You must restrain yourself from eating either the tomatoes or the figs. They are not yet ripe, and if you were to indulge temptation, you would only be disappointed, I'm afraid." She couldn't help but think of that first night with Alan.

He prepared lunch for her every day, made almost entirely from his homegrown produce: kale, carrots, cherry tomatoes (but not the big yellow ones, of course), basil, lemon, bread he had baked himself, goat butter from a farm up in Peñasco.

"What do you do?" he asked on the first day. "When you're not here."

That dreaded question, and she couldn't exactly tell him she was a botanist, now could she? "Oh, I, well, I tend bar up at El…"

"No, no. I don't care where you work. I want to know what you *do*?"

"Oh. Oh, of course," she said. She found herself babbling almost uncontrollably, telling August things she would never tell anyone else, not because they were secret, but because they seemed insignificant, or embarrassing. And he listened. Oh how he listened. She went on and on about the Nia classes she attended every Tuesday and Thursday morning. She revealed her long and unspoken belief that dance was really her true calling, and that had her parents been more prescient and supportive and had she been born with a slightly different body type, she might be living in New York, choreographing and performing in her own contemporary pieces. She spoke about how she liked to ski up the Windsor Trail by herself and cut turns through meadows, the sound muffled all around, in spite of the danger, and afterwards enjoyed coming down from the rush by sitting in a dark and empty bar, sipping a glass of wine, and reading a novel by Lydia Millet or the poetry of Mary Oliver. She did not tell him that she used to be a lawyer. She did not tell him exactly what happened with her marriage.

"And, well, I guess I'm also sort of, well, an artist?" She had never said that before, to anyone. Nor had she shown anyone her creations — collages of photographs that she had manipulated to look like paintings. But it was while creating these works that she felt most fulfilled, most within herself.

"I thought as much," he said. "I could see it in your eyes, in the way you observe things. In your attentiveness."

His tone, in the beginning, carried a hint of condescension. Melissa forgave him that, though; he may not have been the old man that she had originally imagined, but he was probably ten years older than her forty-five. He chose his words carefully when he spoke and he rarely talked about himself. Occasionally moments of his past would bob up to the surface, before sinking back into the depths. Augustus was an actual botanist, he had taught at a university for years, not just some rare plant collector. He focused his research on the extinction of plant species due to climate change, his eyes misting over when he spoke of the death of the last St. Helena olive. Augustus had been married, once, and even had kids, but the marriage had ended in a traumatic way. He was not involved romantically with anyone at the moment. And he was an intensely private person.

Occasionally, when she stopped talking about herself and the conversation threatened to turn in his direction, he pushed it back to her by bringing up some detail about her life that she hadn't consciously revealed to him already. They were mundane details, like the fact that she worshipped Leonard Cohen, or had read *One Hundred Years of Solitude* once a year for the last decade. Two days before he was to depart on his first trip August invited Melissa to stay for dinner and, unprompted, had cooked her favorite type of pasta, with sardines, capers, and olives, had served it with her favorite sancerre, and followed it up with a lemon sorbet that he had made from his own fruit. They ate it in the greenhouse, at a little French cafe table he had set up underneath the fig tree. It was precisely what she desired, transporting her to the Mediterranean even as she was feeling terribly oppressed by the unusually cold and snowy weather. And yet it was also a bit unnerving, as if he could read her mind.

"So, where are you going again?" Melissa asked as she spooned the sorbet onto her tongue. "For your trip, I mean."

"A conference," he said curtly, volunteering no more.

"Okay. But where. What? It's top secret? Some meeting of the Freemason Florists of the World or something?"

He smiled that loin-warming smile of his, and sheepishly spoke: "Nothing like that. I'm going to Bulgaria."

"Bulgaria? What's in Bulgaria?"

"Roses… and a lot of plants. It has remarkable biodiversity, in fact."

"Roses? Oh, I see, Mister Rare Plants himself is going halfway across the world to look at some roses? I don't think so."

August's smile disappeared and he looked away, as if considering something. He looked up toward one corner of the greenhouse roof. He looked back at Melissa. "You are quite the persistent one, aren't you?" he said, the condescension back. "This is just between us, yes?"

"Sure. My lips are sealed." She puckered a little bit, as if tossing him a kiss.

"That's where the philanthropist is who supports my work."

"Work?"

"It's very … complicated… technical stuff."

Melissa's face flushed, but this time it had nothing to do with arousal or passion. It was anger. August was no better than the rest, after all. "I'm not stupid, you know."

"I didn't say that… I, no, no, Melissa. It's just that it's … sensitive."

"Ha! Sensitive? Give me a fucking break, Gus. Explain it to me, then. In, you know, simple terms that even a moronic woman like me can understand."

"Melissa, please… I will tell you everything. In due time."

"Oh, in due time. Just like I can eat the tomatoes and the figs and all that in due time. You mean when I'm 'ripe?' Is that it? I'm not one of your plants. I'm already ripe. I'm so fucking ripe I'm about to fall off the tree and rot into the earth while worms and ants devour my carcass."

August smiled that fucking smile again, then looked down at the table and spoke so softly that Melissa almost couldn't hear: "My work, my life's project, is to create a sort of lifeboat to save all the species threatened by climate change. Some might call it a Noah's Ark for the Anthropocene."

"Huh. So you're going to dig up all the plants and stick them in a giant greenhouse? A biosphere?"

"Not exactly. The plants will be able to stay in place. That's critical. A crested saguaro in a pot in a greenhouse is not the same as a crested saguaro growing in the Sonoran Desert."

"Oh." Melissa started to feel dizzy as the implications sunk in. "This philanthropist must be loaded, eh? Who is it?"

"A Russian…."

"Why Bulgaria if he's Russian? I've never heard of a Russian philanthropist, by the way. I think they have a different word for that?"

August silently cursed himself and looked around again, as if to check to see if the plants were listening to him. "Yes, I suppose you could call Mr. Ivanov an oligarch. He's in Bulgaria because that's where he does business now with all the sanctions on him and his Russian associates."

"Sanctions?"

"Yes. He is, ummm, in the defense industry. And petrochemicals."

"Don't you mean to say that he's an arms dealer and an oil man? And he's going to save plants from global warming? The irony."

"I don't think the irony is lost on him, to be honest. Let's just say that we are looking to the same means to achieve entirely different ends. I can't say anymore. I'm sorry. But you must understand. I have sacrificed everything, literally, for this project. Now we are so close, and I can't afford to jeopardize it … or you."

That is ominous, Melissa thought. The tone of his voice was enough to keep her from pushing it anymore. "Sure. I won't say a thing so long as you promise to make me this meal again."

"Done," he said. That smile came back, and Melissa's innards quivered.

The next day, the final day of training, they transplanted a lime tree together. It was difficult work and August took his shirt off, revealing a trim and fit torso, a line of dark hair leading enticingly from his abs downward. He wore cut off jean shorts, his legs were tan, muscular, coated with reddish brown hair. As he leaned over she caught a glimpse of what looked like a tattoo on his thigh, but then it vanished under his shorts; it seemed so uncharacteristic that she didn't want to ask about it, perhaps afraid of what the explanation might be. By the time they were done, both were tired and dripping with sweat, their odors mingling with the rich smell of earth.

"Here," said August, scooping a handful of dark, loamy soil from the ground. "Smell this."

He held it up to her face with one hand, the other just barely grazing the small of her back. She bent down, closed her eyes, and breathed in deeply, taking in not only the smell of earth, but also his smell – salty and smoky all at once. His mouth almost touching Melissa's ear, August whispered: "Thus doth the kernel, while dry, cover that motionless life. Upward then strives it to swell, in gentle moisture confiding, and, from the night where it dwelt, straightway ascends to light." Her eyes still closed, Melissa felt her cheeks get hot and her nipples harden. Red splotches bloomed pruriently on her neck and chest. She turned slowly to August, closed her eyes, leaned her head back, and offered her lips…

"Okay," he said abruptly as he stood up and stepped away. "I think you're ready. My flight leaves early tomorrow, so take care of my babies. Oh, and remember: don't eat the tomatoes, and stay clear of the Rothschild orchid. Please."

When Melissa arrived at the greenhouse the next morning, she didn't feel like taking care of anything. She was a bit hungover – after leaving the greenhouse the night before, she drank three rose-flavored martinis, in honor of Bulgaria, to drown her sadness and humiliation, ate a frozen pizza to extinguish her palate's pleasant memories of the previous night's dinner, watched *Crazy Ex-Girlfriend* for commiseration, and dug out her vibrator and had to recharge it three times in a futile attempt to temper her lust. Instead of following the daily routine, she slumped down in the dirt and wondered how she could have been so wrong about August. For a moment, she considered just walking out, and letting the plants take care of themselves.

But she needed the cash, and August was paying her twice what she made at the bar, even counting tips. Besides, the tropical microclimate had done wonders for her skin. Her lips were no longer chapped, she didn't need to moisturize, her crow's feet had diminished. Her seasonally affected depression disorder had dissipated. And her libido had been set aflame by the climate, the floral orgy going on all around her, and, yes, by August — tall, lean, smart, confident, witty August of the luscious lips. Oh, August, he whom did not feel the same about her; he whom was more fond of his flowers than his new flower tender. Fuck. Needing exactly that, she had almost texted Alan, the coffee shop boy, but stopped herself because for some weird reason she felt like doing so would be unfaithful to August. What the hell had happened to her? It was awful.

She stood up, did a few karate kicks at the air, and got to work, deadheading here, watering there, but withholding fluid from the tomatoes because, as both August and Goethe had made very clear, doing so makes the fruit that much sweeter. If that were true, then she was getting a lot sweeter, too, and when August returned he'd better watch out. She did the same thing the next day, and the day after that. The plants seemed to do just fine, but they also seemed to be as indifferent to Melissa's presence as August apparently was.

August paced across the concrete at the Santa Fe Railyard, waiting anxiously for the train to Albuquerque to arrive so that he could get on with the first leg of a long trip to southeastern Europe. To say he was agitated would be putting it mildly. He was ablaze. He was angry at himself. He was ready to turn around and walk right back home and ravage Melissa.

It wasn't supposed to be like this. He was supposed to cultivate the asset, nourish her, bring her slowly to an understanding of what she was meant to do. Even August didn't know what she was supposed to do, yet. Recruitment was not in August's job description, but this asset was special, Ivanov had said. The operation had used her without her knowledge to get to someone else, and now they had to repay her.

Repay her by drawing her into this fucking web that seemed to stretch into every corner of every life on the planet.

August was to place the ad and interview applicants until he got the signal — so clumsily relayed by that dimwit Alan via handwritten numbers on the applicant's envelope. When the asset arrived, he was to follow a carefully laid out procedure, remaining detached, objective, dispassionate. And then Melissa walked through that greenhouse door and flipped it all on its head.

From that first day, August had been tortured day and night by images of Melissa: her muscular body; the gentle curve of her ass in those old, worn jeans; her nipples hard under the thin fabric of her shirt; her lips like fruit, full and ripe with expression; and her smell like the sea and an orchid and wood all swirled into one. It had awakened something in him that had long been dormant.

His carnal desires, which were once overflowing, had been stilled by Colette's death. When months passed and then years, and his appetite had yet to return, he felt a little sad, but also relief. He attributed it to age, a natural mellowing of the bodily fire, leaving him free to live a Cartesian life of the mind. And then, just when it seemed that the embers would die out completely, Melissa arrived and dumped high-octane gasoline all over his libido — not only did the flame of lust burn more brightly now than in his youth, but it seemed to be fueled by the intellect, which is part of why Melissa so perturbed him.

Her presence had so confounded him that he spilled far, far too much about Bulgaria, Ivanov, and Operation SNOW. It was an idiotic, possibly deadly slip, even though he hadn't revealed the most sensitive information. If any of his colleagues caught the slightest whiff of his indiscretion, he'd face dire consequences. God knows he'd seen it before. Javier took a knife to the gut in Budapest, Georgi was disappeared years ago, and Colette, oh sweet Colette, shot in the head down in Mexico, her lovely body tossed unceremoniously into the Sea of Cortez, all because she tried to tip off that Tucson reporter. But then, she knew the stakes better than anyone. Colette will be Colette, in death as in life.

The sound of electronic bells clanged through the Railyard, telling August that the RailRunner to Albuquerque, and his ride to the airport, was about to depart. He remembered his goodbye to Melissa the day before, the way she had offered herself up to him, and the hunger he had felt then, so potent that it ached. He longed to turn around, to run back to the greenhouse, to submit to her under the fig tree. But that would be to throw it all away, not just his life's work, but also his life, itself. He had to be strong. Melissa would still be there when he returned. He was sure of that. And the fruit would be sweeter than ever.

He bounded up the steps into the train, as if he had never faltered, settled into his seat, and watched the desert speed past.

2

April 2015

The bee in the pool in the sun in Mexico buzzes its wings, sending tiny ripples through the water. A dove flies over. Sweat drips into my eye. An insect hums in my ear, intent on driving me insane. The sun falls across the smooth curve of my wife's thigh.

I'm on assignment here, in this colonial town in southern Sonora. I'm a journalist, or thought I was. I was supposed to be chasing down an anonymous tip about some crazy weather modification scheme down here. But my editor, Laurel, nixed that one and assigned a story about getting good deals in Mexican towns as a result of all the drug violence, instead. Now I guess I'm a taco writer, a reporter on the carne asada beat. My wife tagged along because she had nothing better to do. We've been here a week, searching for cheap tacos at mealtime, sitting around by the pool in between. It has not been a difficult assignment.

The car goes by. The yellow one, yellow like a cab in New York City, but crawling over the cobblestone streets, dust on its rear window, its hubcaps missing, loudspeakers on top blaring out a refrain, unintelligible.

"What's up with that?" I ask Melissa, my wife, who speaks Spanish better than I. "What are they saying?"

"They're selling things, I think," she says, wondering why I care.

"Like what?" I ask. We have been married for years.

"I don't know," she says. Sometimes we have nothing to say.

"Carne asada?" I ask.

"Maybe. I doubt it."

"Good. Because you can only eat so much carne asada. Do you want another beer?"

Melissa shrugs her shoulders and turns over so that she's lying on her back, topless, her belly and breasts all shiny with sweat. It still gets me, even after all these years — the way her bones swim underneath her flesh, the way her lips look when she is asleep, the mole on her neck just above her clavicle. "Clavicle," I whisper. "Clavicle." I walk over to the house, get a Tecate out of the refrigerator, liking the cold wet that's gathered on the smooth aluminum surface. I slice a piece of lime, pop open the can, and slip the lime in then carry it back to Melissa.

"Hey, do you want me to put some sunscreen on your … on you?"

"No, I'm okay," she says, then sighs. "Yeah, actually, yeah, that would be nice."

She rolls back onto her stomach, saving me from having to hide my erection. I straddle her so I'm sitting on her pillowy round ass, and lightly rub the sunscreen into her freckled, muscular shoulders, giving her a massage in the process. I move surreptitiously down to her lower back. She moans agreeably as I work. I pull her swimsuit bottoms down just a bit, rubbing the sunscreen on the top of her ass, right where the cleft begins. I grease up her pale thighs with the sunscreen, letting a finger brush her sex ever so lightly through her swimsuit. My cock strains against my shorts. It feels like it's going to burst. I move down to her calves, even the bottom of her feet.

I close my eyes and think about the Canadian woman who is reading Roberto Bolaño's *2666*. We saw her again today, when we went to lunch — carne asada tacos of course. Laurel had told me to keep an eye open for her, that we'd see her as soon as we arrived in a public place. And she was right. We were supposed to acknowledge her, to say hi as if we were strangers.

"But we *are* strangers," I told Laurel.

"She is. You're not." And that was that. "She'll give you some advice. But don't ask her for it, just wait. And don't tell Melissa anything."

We saw the Canadian woman the first day in the plaza by the church. And we saw her again, at least once, every day after that. We said hello and exchanged pleasantries, but it wasn't until today, when Melissa was in the store buying some juice, that the Canadian woman gave me any advice: "There's a place on the edge of town," she said. "They sell a mean carne adovada. Go there. And then, tomorrow, when you leave, drive to S** C***** and stay there for the night." I haven't mentioned the exchange to Melissa.

"Hey, honey," I say to Melissa, who lifts her head to take a sip of her beer. "I hear there's a taco stand on the edge of town that sells carne adovada. Should we go there for dinner? We could mix it up on our last night here, yeah?"

"Yeah, sure, whatever."

The car with the loudspeaker is making another round, the voice coming from the speaker has a more urgent tone than before. I look toward the sound, notice the way the light flickers off of the shards of broken glass that line the top of the stone wall surrounding the courtyard surrounding the pool.

"Are you sure they're selling something?" I ask. "What if they're warning us about an earthquake or something? Or inciting revolution? Didn't they just say 'vamanos revoluciones'?"

She says nothing, just turns over, so she's laying on her back again. I smear sunscreen onto the top of her feet, her shins, her knees, her thighs. Her belly is like perfectly proofed ciabatta dough. I sprinkle a few kisses around her navel, run my tongue down to the hollow by her hip, then put some sunscreen there, too, pulling her swimsuit down just enough so that the top of her thick, coarse bush shows. Almost imperceptibly she spreads her legs just a little. I try to ignore it, spreading sunscreen on her belly, my hand pressing up against her first rib, the one that protrudes a bit, then slathering her breasts. Her nipples are hard and have grown darker, so puckered that her aureolas have shrunk to almost nothing. I want to take them into my mouth, to clamp down on them with my teeth. Her hips rise slightly, involuntarily, each time I rub my hands across her breasts.

The car and the blaring voice are back. The tone is more urgent than before.

"Maybe they normally sell things," I say, sleepily. "But today someone hijacked the car and they're leading the revolution as we speak. Listen. Listen. They're saying: Burn the pinche gringos!"

Now she opens her eyes and looks at me. "Do you really want to know what they're saying?"

"Of course. Do tell."

"They're saying that the pinche gringo had better fuck his wife, and now, or else she's going to throw him in the pool."

3

April 2015

The fat man drinks white wine from a glass as big as a fishbowl. He wears dark glasses, a grey porkpie hat, and his arms are so fat that he strains to get the food from his plate to his fork to his mouth. His Mexican wife yells in Spanish at the waiter. She seems angry, but sometimes, down here, it's difficult to tell.

A group of three Americans sit at the corner of the bar. The older one isn't wearing a shirt. Even from across the room, I can see that his eyes are glazed over. The other two are a couple, a plump woman with cowboy boots and too-tight jeans and curly blonde hair, and a man with a red, round face. In unison, all three toss back shots of tequila and laugh.

Another American sits down with the fat man and his Mexican wife and strikes up a conversation about the new winebar in town where they have Coronas for a buck at happy hour. This man, too, is red faced. It seems as if he doesn't really know the couple, but he doesn't seem to care. The Mexican woman replies curtly to him, in English. The fat man just keeps sucking down that wine.

"Cerveza?" the waiter asks me.

"Si," I say. "Negra Modelo."

Melissa orders shrimp cocktail and ceviche and crab tostados, in Spanish.

The fat man continues to scoop up his food without moving his head or neck or body. The Mexican wife has calmed down. She wears gold jewelry and smokes a cigarette. The older of the trio of Americans stumbles outside, and lays down on a white plastic lawn chair on the rocky beach.

We are here because the Canadian woman who reads Roberto Bolaño told me to come here. And I listened to the Canadian woman because Laurel, my boss, told me to. We are on our way back to Tucson after a week in southern Sonora, eating cheap tacos. When I saw the sign for this little town I had told Melissa that we should stop, that I had read about the town somewhere. That's not true. Melissa didn't want to stop, wanted to keep pushing on into the night, to get back to whatever or whomever it was who awaits. "These highways are dangerous at night," I said.

After we pulled off the potholed highway, the road signs led us to a palm-lined avenue that paralleled the beach. This took us to what they called a town, but was really just a row of hotels and American-looking stores. What the cultural landscape lacked, the topography made up for. Rocky, cactus-strewn peaks rose up from the calm waters. "This is like the place where the desert meets the sea," I had said to Melissa. And it is true.

This is also where old gringos come to die. I realize this after we've cruised the strip of highway that passes for a town, and after we've checked into the hotel and sat down under the brittle palm fronds of the bar next to the fat man and the Mexican wife and the three Americans at the bar. It all feels like a bad movie – the kind of movie with Jimmy Buffett covers for a soundtrack. But that's okay, we're not planning on staying long. We'll take a swim in the sea, we'll lie on the rocky beach, we'll drink a shot of tequila or two, we'll sleep here, then we'll go. Maybe we'll see the Canadian woman again and she'll recommend another taco joint.

Melissa is looking out toward the sea. I'm looking at her. She's beautiful. I should tell her that, should stand up and walk around the table, and kiss that mole that sits just above her perfect clavicle. I'm getting hard thinking about it, thinking about where that kiss might lead, about what Melissa and I might do back in the hotel room on the bed that feels like it's made of cardboard. I imagine her on the bed, her legs open, her sex, swollen and wet, welcoming me inside. I imagine her stroking herself hard while I plunge into her, of her muscles spasming as we come in unison. I imagine waking up everyone in the hotel with the thumping of the bed against the wall. If this is a shitty movie, I pray silently to whatever gods preside over this place, let it be a porn flick.

The waiter arrives with the food. It's not bad. The fish is fresh, and the beer is cold. I take a few hungry bites before I realize that Melissa isn't eating. She's looking at me instead in a way that suggests that she has something to say, something besides some comment on the weather, or the shrimp cocktail. I brace myself. Maybe she found out about that thing in the car wash with Laurel. Maybe she's going to tell me how miserable she is with her life, how empty, how she feels like a seaside city. I'm surprised when she says just the opposite: "I've been feeling so good, lately," she says, and my hopes for the hotel room are rekindled. "There's this person, at work. They are smart, witty, and really listen."

"They?" I ask, irritated by her use of the pronoun.

But she is saved from answering by the sound of someone screaming.

We both look through the palm fronds toward the beach. Nothing seems out of the ordinary: A beige blanket of sand, blemished here and there by a body on a towel, skin shiny and baked brown. Maybe the scream is coming from the movie set, I think. But this is no movie, is it? I stand up to get a better look, and see a man in pants and long sleeves trotting in the direction of a scrum of humanity gathered by the water a few hundred yards up the beach. I start walking, following the jogging man.

"What are you doing?" Melissa asks.

"I'm going to see about this," I reply, with as much assurance and authority as I can muster. The group of people are gathered around a woman. She's the one who is screaming, that much is clear, but she looks like she's okay otherwise — no visible wounds, no stingray dangling from her calf. She's pointing at something out in the water: a limp, dark thing slinking back and forth with the waves. It could be her child or her husband. Someone should go out there, I think, and rescue them. Maybe he or she is still alive. I look around for a surfboard or a boat or something I can pilot out to whatever it is, but also know that I'm not going to do it, even if I do find a suitable watercraft. Instead, I walk toward the woman, who has replaced the screaming with weeping. She's wearing a black two-piece bathing suit. She has a good tan. She's American. I consider going to her, offering comfort to my fellow countryman.

The crowd is no longer gathered around the woman. The people are all looking out toward the sea, where a teenaged boy has paddled out and is now pulling the thing back to the shore unceremoniously with a rope, as if he were walking a dog on a leash. When he gets to the shallow water, he untethers the rope from his leg and paddles until he hits the beach with a little thud.

It is a body. It is dead, lying face down in the water, rubbing up against the sand as it bobs rhythmically in the waves. It's a woman, wearing nothing but a tight, dark blue top and and either a skimpy swimsuit or underwear. She's beautiful. I don't know why I notice this, I don't want to notice this, but I do. Her dark hair floats lazily on the water like a stain. Maybe, heartbroken, she'd tossed herself off one of the big cliffs over there, drowned, and washed up here. At first, no one gets close to the body, as though it were a disease. Then, a Mexican man with a big gut pushes through the crowd. His clothing is unkempt and he looks unbearably sad. At first, I think that this must be the woman's father or husband, and that he has been waiting nearby for her since she disappeared. Then I see the glint of the badge, and the holstered gun.

When I get back to the bar, Melissa's still there, poking at the screen of her phone.
"Who are you texting?" I ask.
"No one."
"Oh."
She hasn't eaten anything, but her beer's gone, and she's halfway through mine. I ask the waiter for a tequila, and another beer. Melissa says nothing.
"It was a body," I say. "A woman. She's dead."
The waiter brings the tequila. It burns pleasantly. The beer is cold and I guzzle half of it, then look at Melissa, waiting for something.

Anything. She's still silent. Her phone dings and she looks down at it, smiles at whatever appears there, swipes the message away, and looks back at me as if I were a mere distraction, the ghost of the smile lingering on her lips. "Oh, I see. That's sad."

"Yeah. Murdered. Maybe she killed herself, I don't know." I wave to the waiter and yell across the tables: "Mas tequila por favor!" I catch a glimpse of the red-faced Americans, now obviously drunk. I'll get there, too, I think. I'll get there, too. But for now I'm stuck thinking about what happened at the beach.

After inspecting the body and then the crowd for a few moments, the cop had bent down and surveyed the woman's lifeless body without touching it. Everyone moved back a little, except for me. He pulled some latex gloves from his shirt pocket, and pulled them expertly onto both hands, which were big and brown and riddled with scars. Then, carefully, he rolled the Canadian woman who liked to read Roberto Bolaño over and repeated the visual inspection, his hands gently prodding at her ribs and stomach, as if to wake her up from a nap. He reached up with his hand, touched her face, and ran his fingers through her hair, like a lover would.

"What the fuck is it with this country," I had muttered quietly, the sound of the waves making my voice inaudible as I took a step back.

The man had stopped then and looked right at me. "Just like the others," he said, in English, and I didn't know if he was talking about me, or the dead Canadian woman. And then, while still looking in my direction, he inserted his pinky finger into a hole in her head, just above the left ear. Feeling sick, I turned to walk away. But as I did my eyes fell on something I hadn't noticed before. On her inner thigh was a tattoo. It looked like lettering. I stopped and knelt down to get a closer look. Familiar, yet indecipherable: СНЯГ. It was Russian, maybe, or some sort of code. The cop saw me looking. I wanted to explain that I was trying to understand the tattoo, not looking at the curve of her thigh, and that maybe I had seen one like it before, but I couldn't remember where. "Just like the others," the cop said. "Just like the others." At that I had walked hurriedly back to Melissa, who was still in the bar, but had not waited for me.

After my second tequila shot, I feel the warmth in my chest, a tingle behind my eyeballs. A strand of hair hangs over Melissa's face. I stand up and reach over to push it away and as I do I see the message on her phone. I tuck the hair behind her left ear. "This place is beginning to grow on me," I say. "Why don't we stay another day or two?"

She doesn't look at me. She says nothing.

I reach into the breast pocket of my shirt and pull out the folded piece of paper. The taco vendor from the night before, the one selling carne adovada out on the edge of town, had handed it to me along with three tacos and a Tecate. I thought it was some third-world notion of what a napkin should be, but when I saw the look in the taco vendor's eyes I slipped it into my pocket while Melissa wasn't looking and forgot about it, until now. I unfold the paper, and then unfold it again, and then again. It is a much larger sheet of paper than I had anticipated. It is covered from side to side, top to bottom, with tightly packed columns of very small, but elegant, handwriting. It takes a moment for my mind to adjust to reading the tiny script, written in a fine tipped pen. It is a list of names. Dozens of them. Hundreds. Each name has a five digit number following it. I recognize some of the names: a prominent American businessman, real estate developer, and reality television star; a politically progressive actress; a prominent novelist; a reporter for the *New York Times*; a senator from Kentucky. Others seem familiar, but I can't quite place them. It's like some *Who's Who* of modern American culture, and has no special meaning to me. My attempt to read every single name falters about a third of the way through as my eyes blur over. Maybe I need glasses.

"Hey, Melissa, take a look at this list. Is there some pattern or something? Recognize anyone? I mean besides the obvious celebrity types."

She sighs and takes the paper from my hand, holds it up close to her face and then extends her hand out as if it were a zoom lens as she tries to focus. Her lips move as she reads the names, then her forehead crinkles up.

"What's your boss's name? The one you have a crush on?"

I feel myself blush, briefly remember the car wash incident, sweat beads on my neck. "Laurel. Laurel Weinberger. What makes you think I have a crush on her?"

"She's on here."

"That doesn't mean I have a crush on her. Let me see."

"Wait a minute, wait a minute." She's studying the paper more intently now. "Uhhh, Malcolm?"

"What. Who now?"

"You're on the list, too. Where did you get this?" Now she hands it to me and points to my name and Laurel's. I start at the beginning again and scan every name. It takes a while. Mary Aitken is there, as is Peter Simons, my childhood buddy. And, at the very bottom, in the lower right hand corner, it says "Malcolm Brautigan 06554."

I fold the piece of paper, put it back in my pocket and wave to the waiter again. He knows what I want before I even ask.

4

"At least the engine sounds good." That's what I'm thinking as I drive my 1969 Rambler American through the wide streets of Tucson on a Tuesday evening. It is hotter than shit, but the Steely Dan emanating from the brand new speakers sounds as crisp and cool as the air inside the car, courtesy of the Rambler's patented desert-only air conditioning system. Next to me sits Laurel Weinberger, my boss, and I am truly freaking out in all kinds of ways.

As you may have gathered by now, my name is Malcolm Brautigan, and I'm the environment and science reporter for the *Tucson Tribune*. Laurel is the news editor, meaning she gives me my assignments and edits my work. She is smart as hell and intolerant of my particular brand of wonky reporting and is a kick-ass, if somewhat cruel, editor. She's also sexy as all hell, what with those big black-framed glasses, that intellect, that explosion of frizzy black hair, her flirtatious wit, and that way of walking across the newsroom that scrambles my innards every time.

Yeah, I know, with the Steely Dan, and the cool car, and the desert-only action, all topped off with the hottest babe this side of the Gila River sitting right beside me, I should be on cloud nine. The problem is, Laurel Weinberger is a clean freak. And my car? Well, I haven't exactly stayed on top of the janitorial duties when it comes to Romeo the Rambler. It's just not one of my things. The back seat, which conveniently folds down to create a queen-sized clearing, is piled high with three half-empty wine bottles, twelve Budweiser cans, and a bag of Doritos that seems to be oozing crumbs into the rest of the vehicle. My wife, Melissa, avoids riding in the car even when it's clean, for all kinds of reasons; when it's in this state I usually don't even allow people to see the thing, let alone ride in it. And now Laurel's sitting here, trying really hard not to touch anything.

I guess the whole thing started this morning, when I got to work and checked my voicemail. Someone — a woman with an accent that I couldn't place — had left a tip, anonymously. It took me five minutes to listen to the whole thing, and was detailed enough, and strange enough, that I had to listen to it three times to get it all down. She claimed that there was some top-secret climate modification experiment underway in the mountains above Alamos, a little town in southern Sonora, Mexico. The project's objective was to stave off global-warming-caused extinction of a species of cactus that grows only on one slope, of one mountain, outside of Alamos.

Now, I don't fall for every harebrained tip that comes my way. But this tipster gave a number of details that could be verified, and there was something about her tone that lent her credibility. So I spent most of the day writing up a pitch and, just before Miller-Time, delivered it to Laurel, emphasizing the fact that I was going to Mexico for vacation, anyway, so the *Tribune* didn't need to pay my expenses. It seemed like a slam dunk. But as I was getting ready to head home, Laurel stopped me — physically held up her hand and stiff-armed me in the chest, in fact. "You can't write that story," she said.

"What? Why the hell not? Look, I'm going to Mexico anyway…."

"Give me a ride home and I'll explain."

"Give you a ride? What? I … well, you see, my car is, ummm, I don't think…"

"Shut up, Malcolm. I saw you drive in this morning, even though you insist on parking way across the lot. Go get your car, fire up the air conditioner, and pick me up out front in five."

I couldn't really say no, which is why Laurel is now sitting next to me, on my blue bench seat, eyeing that moldy thing on the dashboard nervously, as "Hey, Nineteen" oozes out of those speakers oh so smooth, and I say, probably for the first time in my life and for reasons that I can only explain as coming from some divine source: "Hey, do you mind if I stop at the car wash, this thing's a mess?" I pause and select my next words carefully. "A friend of mine borrowed it and trashed it. I hate driving in a dirty car."

Laurel doesn't smile, or even pause. She only says, in that icy, businesswoman's manner, "I know a great car wash." She gives me directions and I see her relax a little and settle back into the box springs of the bench seat, and when she does her blouse crinkles up a bit between buttons, giving me a clear look at the soft skin of her right breast. I veer into oncoming traffic, but she doesn't seem to notice. I've forgotten about the anonymous tip and my pitch, and she seems to have done the same. Up on the right I see what looks like a car wash, and Laurel puts her hand on my thigh. I'm wearing shorts, even though it's a work day, because I'm a journalist, and we all dress like slobs. "There it is," she says. The hand stays. In fact, it starts moving up towards my crotch, very, very slowly. Despite the cold air blowing from the vents, I start to sweat. Profusely.

I pull up next to the vacuums and jump out. I grab armfuls of garbage and toss them into the dumpster, insert some coins into the slot, then unravel the long, obscene hose and go to work. Laurel gets out, leans against the car, and lights up a cigarette — yet another surprise. At one point I'm down on my knees, really sucking up stuff from under the seat, including an old condom wrapper — a leftover from the Eliza days, and one of the reasons Melissa doesn't like the car — and I feel a weird tingling at the back of my neck. When I look up I see that Laurel is staring right at my ass. This is getting strange.

We get back in the car and pull up to the automated pay center. I open the ashtray and pull out a handful of quarters and deposit some. Just as I am about to push the "econo-wash" button, Laurel stops me, again with her hand on my thigh, only this time her pinky is perilously close to my sex. "Wait," she says, handing me her credit card. "Use this, and select the super duper deluxe jumbo wash. It lasts a long time."

I don't argue. I push the button, then I slowly pull Romeo the Rambler into the car wash bay. Laurel's hand still rests absentmindedly on my thigh when the car comes to a stop, and the second the jets start spraying water onto the windows, her long fingers drift up into my shorts so that her nails brush against my balls. And as soon as the detergent starts sudsing up on the windows, she reaches further up and takes hold of my penis, which is already painfully hard. I am afraid to look at her, or move, or do anything besides keep my hands on the wheel and stare directly at the windshield.

"I'm hot," I blurt, watching her reflection in the window, her lips slightly parted, her eyes sleepy looking, and her right hand, the one that is not in my shorts, down the front of her skirt, moving in a gentle, rhythmic motion.

"I gathered that," she replies, her fingers deftly sliding across the shaft of my throbbing penis. "Now shut up and kiss me."

She pulls my mouth to hers, almost violently, and our lips, teeth, and tongues engage in a crazed battle. As she leans over me in such a way that I can reach up the back of her blouse and deftly unsnap her bra, I thank God for bench seats.

As cycle number two begins, my mouth finds her nipples, erect between my lips. My hand slips up her smooth thigh. I'm a little surprised to see she has a tattoo there, but I'm too close to make it out, and don't really care about that right now, anyway. She arches her back and lifts her ass off the seat so I can pull her underwear off and I gently caress her vulva, and circle one finger around her clitoris while another explores even wetter regions. My mouth meanders leisurely from every little freckle to every little mole as if following the little country roads in the forgotten corner of some Western state — over the gentle hill of her belly down into the valley next to her hip bone. I linger there for a while, my lips barely touching her skin. Laurel Weinberger, however, is not interested in the scenic route. She is a goal-oriented freeway girl and she doesn't hide her impatience with my meandering. She grabs my hair and pushes my face into her sex. I celebrate as I deeply inhale her perfume and savor the coarseness of her pubic hair against my cheeks.

With my left hand I part her lips, exposing her clitoris, and my tongue quickly flicks against the fleshy, engorged fruit. She lets out a small groan, and shudders when my finger enters her and caresses lightly. My tongue finds a rhythm that matches the slow rotation of her hips. She thrusts her sex against my face, but I hold on, sucking harder on her clitoris, now so swollen it feels like it will burst in my mouth like an overripe cherry on the Fourth of July. Her engine is revved and she is barreling down the fast lane straight into Orgasm-town. And when I dip my thumb into her wetness, and slide it down below her pussy, and rub it up against her asshole, circling with the same rhythm in which her hips moved, it is like flipping a hidden switch under the dashboard. Her pubis bucks against me and a deep hiss of pleasure escapes from her clenched teeth as I bare down with tongue, lips, fingers, and thumb. Her gyrations force her head back into the window handle, and the window slides open just enough that a mist of cold water hits us just as the second wave of orgasm crashes over her.

I come up for air, my face covered in her juices. I'm stunned and baffled and disoriented, certain that if Laurel were even to wave a finger within a few inches of my sex, I would come violently. Involuntarily I shrink away from her as she moves toward me.

"Don't be scared," she says, slowly pulling my shorts off, laughing a little as my erection leaps free of the fabric. She pulls a condom from her purse, opens the package, slides it gently onto me. Maybe that will help me last a little longer. She gets on her knees and straddles me, gently guiding me inside of her warmth.

"Holy sweet Jesus," I mutter, as she moves oh so slowly, up, down, and in circles.

"Don't move," she says. "And don't come until I tell you to."

I take her seriously, and do what she says. After all this is the woman who, just yesterday, told me that if I didn't start using the Oxford comma I'd end up working in a Taco Bell on the southside, fucking the assistant manager who had been scooping refried beans and guacamole from a can all day. I meditate, concentrating on the vision of refried beans, and somehow manage to resist all the forces that are compelling me to thrust into her. She's moving erratically, her pubis grinding against mine. My eyes are clenched shut. Little moans are coming from the back of her throat. I feel like I'm going to implode. She leans forward, offering her nipple to my mouth, and screams: "Bite."

I take the gumdrop between my teeth and bite. Not too hard, but hard enough, sucking at the same time. It's too much. I can feel the current of electricity moving through my pelvis, into my shaft, and then the sharp shock of release. I spasm, buck, cry out, mutter something about semicolons. Thankfully she is coming, too. Maybe I won't get fired, after all.

She's still panting as she climbs off of me and leans up against the passenger side door. Within moments, the dry cycle fades away, and the big green light flashes on. I see in the rearview mirror that a car is waiting for us.

"Drive," says Laurel. "Now."

I do just that, and am nearly blinded by the afternoon sunlight as I drive out of the car wash bay, my shorts still around my knees, the condom still sheathing my still-erect sex, and my ass sticking to the blue vinyl seat. I pause at a stoplight to get my bearings and pull up my shorts. Laurel buttons up her blouse and from the corner of my eye I watch with sadness as the last sliver of her nakedness disappears.

"About that tip you got," she says in her office tone of voice as I pull up in front of the house where she lives. "There was no tip. There is no project near Alamos. And there is no story. Drop it. Understand?"

"But… this is right up my alley, Laurel. I even know some people from Silverton who are into this cloud seeding and stuff. Good sources for the science side of things. I mean, it's crazy shit. It's like chemtrails or something."

She looks me in the eyes in a way that frightens me. "I'll tell you what. Go to Mexico. Find out how badly the murders and violence are affecting the tourist industry. More importantly, search out the good deals, the discounts they are offering to entice people to risk decapitation to get a cheap hotel room or whatever. A travel story. Something easy, light."

"I'm not a travel writer, Laurel…"

"Now you are. Take Melissa with you. We'll pay all of your expenses. Stay somewhere nice. Treat your wife like she deserves for once."

I feel myself blush, a sudden onset of guilt washing away the post-coital glow. "You're not gonna tell her, are you?"

"I hope I don't need to, Malcolm. Do you understand?"

"I think so. Yeah, yeah, I get it. I'm a travel writer. I'll be on the cerveza and carne asada beat. Is that what you want?"

"That's what I want. And that thing in the car wash? It never happened." Her tone is so flat, so cold, so harsh, that I actually believe her. I pull away slowly, turn up the Steely Dan, and admire the shiny finish on my car as the sun reaches through the orange haze for the jagged horizon.

5

November 2005

*Albedo is a non-dimensional, unitless quantity that indicates how well a sur-
face reflects solar energy. Albedo varies between 0 and 1. Albedo commonly refers
to the "whiteness" of a surface, with 0 meaning black and 1 meaning white. A
value of 0 means the surface is a "perfect absorber" that absorbs all incoming
energy. Absorbed solar energy can be used to heat the surface or, when sea ice is
present, melt the surface. A value of 1 means the surface is a "perfect reflector"
that reflects all incoming energy.*
  — National Snow and Ice Data Center

"So, albedo is like libido? They're both good."
  — Malcolm Brautigan

"So, wait," I say to Mary Aitken, who sits uncomfortably
close to me in the offices of the *Dandelion Times* newspaper, " is albedo
a good thing or a bad thing?"

"It's good. It's reflectiveness. Snow naturally has a high albedo,
meaning the sunlight bounces off and the snow sticks around a while
longer. Dust diminishes albedo."

Mary Aitken is a snow scientist, and she is in the tiny, snowy
mountain town of Silverton, Colorado, for several months to study
the affects of dust on snow. Every spring, almost without fail, the

winds come to the Four Corners region and lift up huge plumes of dust from the overgrazed and desiccated deserts of Utah and Arizona, and carry that dust north and eastward into Colorado. The sky and air becomes tinted with orange, visibility is cut down, eyes and nostrils collect chunky orange gunk. When the slow-moving dust storm hits the mountains, the dust settles out onto the snow and turns it a brown-orange color, making the already bleak mountain spring even grimmer. It also decreases the snow's albedo, or reflectiveness, meaning that the intense high-altitude sunlight is absorbed by the snowpack rather than getting bounced back, causing the snow to melt more quickly. That, in turn, exacerbates drought conditions down low, which leads to more dust, which leads to faster snowmelt — a feedback loop if there ever was one.

"Got it. Albedo sounds like libido. Both are good."

"Exactly," she says, smiling.

Mary has an office in the old Miners Union Hospital building just down the hall from the *Dandelion Times,* which I own. Both of us frequently work late. I'm trying to survive the nuclear winter of my love affair with Eliza Santos, and work is a good distraction. Mary is married to a guy named David, who stayed in Boulder to work rather than accompany his wife on this temporary posting, and so home for her is a lonely, cold room in the Benson boarding house. Our offices are a good refuge, even if the building does happen to be haunted by those who died within these walls, the victims of flu, silicosis, mine cave-ins, prematurely exploded dynamite, you name it. Mary's office is dark, dingy, and north-facing; mine's on the top floor, with big, south facing windows, and has more space. So it was only natural that Mary would set up shop here with me, so that we can keep each other company as we sit hunched over our respective screens.

I never considered Mary anything other than an office mate and, in a way, a colleague. But tonight there is something in the air. Her smile is like electricity. Her green eyes are bright, and linger on mine for longer than usual. Her long hair spills across her back. I notice, for the first time, the freckles on her chest, where her shirt falls open. "Well, I'd better get back to work," I say, maybe a little too brusquely. She isn't having it.

"Speaking of libido, you're in a relationship, right? Do you and Eliza still… Is the passion still there?"

"Uhhh, well, we're kind of taking a break? Eliza moved down to Santa Fe. Maybe it's just temporary. Maybe not. I don't know. We still hang out, and yeah, we still … Why do you ask?"

"I don't know, it's just that I feel like David's libido has been diminished. He doesn't seem that interested. Is that age? Or what? Do men lose it after a while?"

"No. No, they don't. We don't. Believe me. I mean, sometimes I wish it would go away. The desire. But it doesn't."

"Huh?"

"But I'm not saying that that means anything. Everyone's got their own thing going on. I'm sure David will come around."

"I'm not so sure about that. I've tried. And in my desperation I've become the neglected wife of my worst nightmares."

"How so?"

"It's pathetic. I bought frilly lingerie, sex toys, books of erotica. All pretty much useless, except I did find a pretty good vibrator, by the way. I just wish it had some kind of remote control."

I catch myself with my mouth hanging open, a bit of drool forming on my lip. "Wow. That sucks. Sorry."

"It's probably not as bad as I'm making it out to be. I mean, the guy's not dead. If I catch him when he's not too tired and go down on him for a bit he's good for a quick fuck, which is better than nothing, especially with my new toy to finish me off. It's just that I'm getting tired of doing all the work."

What the hell am I supposed to say to this?

"Okay," she says. "I'll let you get back to it."

Yeah, right. Now I am haunted not only by the ghosts, but by images of a frustrated Mary Aitken trying to get her husband to hump her. I'll never get anything done. For the next week or so I spend as much time in the office as possible, drinking my morning coffee there, taking dinner from the Drive-In there. I tell myself that I'm doing it because I'm devoted, and because I want the *Times* to be the best it can be, but I'm no idiot. The real reason is to be close to Mary. To what end, I'm not really sure. I'm not going to make the moves on her, no way. It's not really my style, for one thing. I'm shy, and usually let the woman make the first move. I know I've thrown away opportunities as a result, but it's better not to get laid than to get laid and realize afterward that she didn't really want it.

There's another niggling little fact: She's married. I may not even know David, and his lack of desire for Mary may confound me, but I still don't want to do that to him. I've been on the wrong side of infidelity before, and I can tell you, it sucks. Even now, years after the fact, I occasionally find myself seized by images of Eliza getting fucked by that guy back in Chicago. The visions arouse, on the one hand, and send slivers of repulsion into my chest, on the other. The combination is enough to make me violently ill. I do not want to be a character in David's similar visions.

I always work late on Thursday nights, because that's the day I put the newspaper to bed, meaning I finish it up, do a final proofread, and send the digital file to the printer. It's a Thursday night, a couple weeks after the albedo-libido conversation, and we are both working, but also sharing a bottle of Scotch to help the creative juices flow more freely, I suppose. Mary hasn't been around much, says she's been busy out in the field, setting up new instrumentation, that sort of thing.

"Instrumentation? I ask. "For what?"

"Sensors, thermometers, you know, boring stuff."

"Oh. So, what's the point, anyway? I mean of your research. Dust makes snow melt faster. You've figured that out. So what now?"

"Well, I'm a scientist, so I'm not supposed to think about that. It's just science for the sake of science on one level. But also, what we've learned can help water managers forecast snow melt and that sort of thing. It's got practical applications."

"Yeah, I don't know. I guess I understand why someone might study how a pesticide causes cancer, because then you can get rid of the pesticide, or whatnot. But understanding how dust melts snow? It's not like you can get rid of the dust. You can't solve this disease."

She pauses for a moment, considering something. "Is this off the record?"

"Of course."

"I need your word that you won't mention any of this to anyone."

"I won't. Lips are sealed. Dead man talk. Seriously."

"To go back to your analogy, the disease isn't dust. The dust is a symptom that leads to other symptoms. The disease is global warming."

"My point exactly. You can't cure global warming. I mean, sure, theoretically you can stop emitting greenhouse gases, but it's getting a little late for that. And here you are — and I don't mean any disrespect — looking at dust."

"My research goes beyond the way dust affects snow. I'm also looking at how dust affects the weather, in general. Do these big spring dust storms seed the clouds, causing more precipitation to fall? Do dust and particulates from Asia that go way up into the atmosphere provide a sort of shade, thus negating a bit of the greenhouse effect? What if we could use artificial means to increase the albedo of the upper atmosphere?"

"Oh. But I thought the Center for Snow ..."

"... focuses mainly on dust on snow. Sure. I don't only work for them. My, umm, extracurricular research is part of another global project. It's funded by someone else."

"Someone else?"

"It's called Operation SNOW, and I really shouldn't be talking about it."

"Cloud seeding? Negating the greenhouse effect? Is this like, weather control or something? Like chemtrails? What's the saying? He who controls the weather, controls the world?"

"Yeah, yeah, like chemtrails. That's the ticket. Let's talk about something else. How's things with Eliza?"

"Terrible." I take a big gulp of Scotch, right out of the bottle. "She's finished with me. I wanted to go down this weekend to visit, but she says she's too busy. I think she's probably found someone else."

"Maybe it's the dust."

"Ha! Yeah, I wish. And you and David?"

"The same. I went back to Boulder for the weekend, and he was even less responsive than usual. Do you think he's having an affair?"

I shrug my shoulders. I have thought about her constantly for the last week. I have dreamed of bathing her body in kisses. The image of Mary Aitken and her vibrator tortures me. I even wrote a poem about the freckles on her chest. No fucking way am I going to let her read it, though.

Our rolling office chairs have somehow moved perilously close to one another, as if magnetized. I am trembling. She reaches her hand up and brushes a strand of hair away from my eye. I feel myself leaning into her hand like a cat into a caress. I open my eyes to find her staring at me with those eyes. She kisses me then, very gently, taking my lip between hers and squeezing lightly. Then again. And again. And then it is a real kiss, mouths and tongues and teeth melting together, her hands, hungry, on my back, in my hair, pressing on my chest. I tentatively put my hand on her breast, savor the weight of it. She reaches down to unclasp my belt, my belly spasming at her touch. I allow myself to imagine what comes next.

Then her phone rings, and we both jump back.

"Fuck fuck fuck," she says, looking at the screen. "It's Ivanov. I'm sorry, I…" She jumps up from her chair, and runs out into the dark hallway, talking into the phone with a different voice, a different accent altogether as she runs down the stairs to where I can no longer make out her words. I won't see her again for many years.

6

Editor's note: *The following is a transcription of an audio recording that was sent anonymously to Malcolm Brautigan when he was a reporter at the* Tucson Tribune. *It is believed to be the voice of Augustus S. Lavender, recounting the beginnings of Operation SNOW.*

Voice 1 (unidentified): Can you please tell us about how you came to be the project director for Operation SNOW? Begin on the night you were recruited. It was in Athen, wasn't it?

Voice 2 (Augustus S. Lavender): Yes, yes, okay then, from that night in Athens. That was in July of 2005. This is how it happened:

The waitress brings us our drinks. The glasses are cold. The waitress's jeans sit low on her hips, her stretchy black t-shirt sits high, drops of perspiration cling to the fuzz of her lower back like dew. Colette and I both stare as she approaches, and as she saunters away.

We are in Athens. It is July. It is sweltering. This was Colette's idea, of course, to come to Athens with all its humanity, history, the smells, the noise, the heat not only beating down from above, but also from the pavement, the stone, the monuments. I would have preferred to recover from my botanical conference under an umbrella, on a beach, on an island, slurping frappes, bobbing around in the sea, sipping Ouzo and Retsina, licking salt water off of her body, and eating grilled octopus. But Colette finds that to be dull, something to be done when we're ninety, maybe, but not now. Not when there's so much life to live. That's how she is.

For so long we have been caught up in day to day life, and cooped up in the small town where we live that just the din of all the voices and dishes clinking together and the music in the background and the energy and the cacophony of multiple conversations is like a tonic. We sit alone on a low couch in a dark corner, talking about places we may someday live: Mexico, Paris, Marseille, Istanbul, maybe even Athens. There is no order or direction to the conversation, it just meanders like the wind.

We haven't talked like this in some time. At home, our words dwell on the mundane and the practical. After the kids go to bed, and when the house is finally quiet, we become awkward. As though, after thirteen years together, there is nothing left to say. Of course, it's not like that – there's plenty of words each day to fill up another day with talk. And my mind whirls relentlessly with a constant stream of words, especially when all I want is peace. If it's not words, it's images. The kind that keep me up at night while my heart pounds with disaster. For whatever reason, I don't let these words out.

Tonight, though, something has surrendered inside. And we speak and are silent at the same time. Our hands touch one another lightly. Colette smolders with sexuality, as she so often does; her cheeks are red, her eyes sparkle, her lips like overripe strawberries. How can it be that a man can desire his wife so fervently after so many years? I imagine taking her out back, into the closed stairwell, pushing her up against the wall, and fucking her as though she were a stranger with nothing to lose. But I don't move. Tonight my desire is a languid one; I could stay here on this couch drinking and listening to my wife and watching the waitress forever.

Before we came to Athens we were in Sofia, Bulgaria, at a conference of botanists, where I presented not one, but two papers relating to the extinction crisis. I study plants, specifically species that are on the brink of vanishing. I am not an academic, however. I like to put my hands in the dirt, as they say. And I like to solve real world problems. I spend most of my time searching for ways to rescue the species that might otherwise go missing, to help the immobile uproot themselves and flee from the looming climate catastrophe as refugees, and to replant them in a more amenable climate. More controversially, my colleagues and I devise ways to create micro-climates that resist the global warming urge, or fiddle with a plant's DNA just enough to allow it to survive, but not to alter its identity. This tinkering with natural systems is sometimes referred to as geo-engineering and GMOs, respectively. Our critics are many. We have been spit upon, had our fields and laboratories burned, our lives threatened. We shouldn't play God, they tell us, we shouldn't be poking around where nature should be left to run its course, we are heretics. They are missing the point. We are nature; nature is us. There is more plastic in the sea than kelp, more pharmaceuticals in the streams than algae. Splicing a fish gene with that of a tomato is no less natural than evolution itself.

We order another drink. This time, though, when the waitress walks away, and my eyes follow the tattoo on her lower back, my gaze falls on another pair of eyes. His eyes are dark. His hair is dark, too, and brushes against his neck like a girl's. He sits at the bar. He is beautiful, his lips smooth and lush. His gaze is so intense that he must be the waitress's lover, and he's warning me away. Then he stands up, and approaches us.

"Hi," he says, looking first me, then Colette, in the eyes. "I couldn't help overhearing your conversation. You were speaking of Marseille, no?" He has full lips, dark olive skin and speaks with a slight accent. I know without looking at her that my Colette's cheeks are even redder now, and warmth is creeping through her belly and thighs. A twinge of jealousy pokes at me, along with suspicion: How could he have possibly heard what we were saying from way over there?

"Sit down," Colette says. "Please."

My fantasies for the night — of going back to our rental apartment and making slow, sweaty love while the flimsy curtains blow back and forth in the window — fade. We will be here for hours, Colette and her new friend gabbing on and on into the night. Oh well. It's an excuse to drink more of this fabulous wine, to eat more of those little fried anchovies straight out of the sea. Colette will be Colette.

Back in Bulgaria Colette did her best to join the other spouses on daily outings while their significant others prattled on about plants in the conference rooms at the Russian Cultural Center. She spent the first day on a walking tour of Sofia's archaeological wonders, and the second on a trip to the Rila Monastery, most of which was spent cooped up in a bus where botanists' wives prattled on about their impotent husbands. It drove her mad, and on day three she alighted off by herself, wandering among the towering, brutalist "panelki" apartment buildings put up en masse during the Communist era. Shocked by the sight of so many stray dogs, she rented a van, bought fifty kilos of dog food from an outdoor market, hired four Roma kids to help her, and drove around town feeding the homeless dogs. On day four she checked out the decaying, beautiful buildings of the old Jewish neighborhood. Judging by the grafitti it had become the white nationalists' district in more recent times. So she went to one of the little hardware stores, bought several cans of spray paint, and painted over or refashioned the numerous swastikas she found scrawled on the building walls.

Somehow she also managed also to create an Instagram sensation called "LostInTranslation," in which she captured linguistic surprises encountered on the streets of Sofia (a former dancer, Colette is now a translator and interpreter). Her images include: A woman walking out of a store called "KINKY" with a t-shirt that reads, "Wine Me Dine Me Sixty-Nine Me;" a younger woman in a restaurant called "Nana's Face," wearing a knit sweater with the words "Fuck A Suck;" a gangly kid, probably no older than eight, with a t-shirt emblazoned, in big, black letters: "My vagina tastes like Coca-Cola." My personal favorite was the "Intellectual Curling Iron" she found in a trinket shop.

On day five she came back from her daily wanderings and as we ate our shopka salads and sipped ice-cold rakia, she pulled up her skirt to show me the tattoo she had gotten that day on her inner thigh. It said СНЯГ, which is Bulgarian for "snow," and she did it in honor of my pie-in-the-sky project — the big one that probably never would be realized. It was a sweet and ridiculously sexy gesture, and later that night I would trace the Cyrillic letters with my tongue before moving on to warmer, wetter climes. But first she insisted we go to the so-called "Mafia Bar." A Bulgarian botanist colleague of mine had warned me away from the place, just as he had cautioned me not to take the mafia taxis, which meant Colette was instantly drawn to it. We arrived to find a Maserati, a Bentley, three Porsches, and a Lamborghini parked outside, illegally. The bar was actually part of the lobby of an ostentatious hotel: shiny black and white faux marble, copious crystal chandeliers, the liquor shelf backlit with pastel colors. As we entered via a revolving door, it felt as if we were stepping into Liberace's wardrobe.

The clientele was also very distinct looking. All of the men's heads, without exception, were shaved to stubble, and they wore black t-shirts ripping at the seams, black blazers, mirrored sunglasses. The women — dressed in stillettos plastered with glitter and tight, short dresses, all seemed to have been engineered, their lips, cheeks, breasts, bellies, butts, calves, and noses altered in some way, fat removed or silicone added. Colette not-so-subtly remarked on the eery similitude between cantaloupes, the biceps of nearly all of the men there, and the breasts of the women at their sides. "It's as though Dr. Z got a volume discount on a single variety of implants," she said, far too loudly, referring to the plastic surgeon whose billboards loomed over the city's main boulevards. I tried to shush her, to get her to whisper her insults, at least. I, for one, did not want to be the one to find out whether the cantaloupe-arms were real or fake. Afterward, our bodies buzzing with rakia and adrenalin, she dragged her key along the length of the Maserati, leaving a long scratch in the yellow paint, and setting off the alarm. I grabbed her arm and pulled her away while berating her and laughing giddily; people had been assassinated for less.

Colette will be Colette, and life with her is never dull.

The man sits down, perhaps a little close to Colette for my taste. He once lived in Marseille, he says. It is like music there. I speak up, trying to appear social and animated and pro-active, and tell him we hope to live in Marseille one day, too, or maybe Sicily, or even Athens. That we are longing for that sort of experience.

"Yes," he says, "I imagine with your line of work you can live wherever you'd like."

I may be comfortably buzzed from the wine, but I am certain we have told him nothing about our work or our lives. I glance over at Colette to see if she's noticed. Splashes of red have bloomed on her neck and chest; this is not a sign of suspicion or alarm, but of arousal and desire. I can't help but wonder if Colette wasn't up to more in Sofia than stifling nazis, feeding the strays, and mocking organized crime bosses. Perhaps she arranged this rendezvous in advance; perhaps the two lovers will lure me to the Acropolis and toss me over the edge before running off to the Greek island at which I longed to be.

Before my imagination runs amok, however, he slides into a soliloquy, telling us about his *grand amor*. He once met a Canadian dancer from Montreal while she was touring in Rome. She called herself Nikki, but her name was Nicoletta. He fell in love. She would travel to one city, then stay for months, performing with the local company. Then move on. He followed her to Budapest, then Moscow, then Marseille.

"Our love was like a storm," he says. "You know, in the summer, on the hot afternoons, when the clouds tower up above the earth like monsters, and the wind bends even the sturdiest trees, and you can feel the hair all over your body standing on end because the air is rich with electricity? That's how it was at first. Then, later, while we were in Marseille, the clouds opened up violently."

He stares off into space for a moment. The silence is not awkward. I feel like he must have learned English from reading novels or watching *Masterpiece Theatre* back in the seventies.

"I'm afraid I am a very jealous man. I despise that about myself. But a great French novelist – a woman, I can't remember her name – who had many lovers, was terribly jealous, too. Once, a reporter asked her about that. And she said that jealousy is just a by-product of passion. If you have no jealousy, then you have no love…"

He looks my wife in the eyes as he speaks. The rest of the world dissolves. I take another long drink of Ouzo to feel the cold burn.

"Every day that she was rehearsing, and at nights in performances, I was inflamed. My chest felt like it would explode. So, each night, when she returned, I couldn't stop myself. We fought like thunder. I was sure she was in love with Mikhail, the choreographer; he was so beautiful… One night, I was drunk. I went to his apartment in an ancient building; it was spring and so warm and the night was alive, with Africans strolling through the street everywhere. Oh, but I was on fire. I went to his house and burst inside and I screamed at him and screamed until I collapsed in exhaustion… When I awoke, I was in his bathtub, he was bathing me. Touching my skin, my nipples, my sex, so gently but also with hunger. I had never been touched like that before…"

Colette and I have sunken into the couch, mesmerized.

"Oh," he says, "I'm sorry, I must be boring you."

"No, no, no, please go on," I say.

"Well, of course, Mikhail and I fell in love. Nikki went back to the States. Mikhail and I began fighting, too, for the same reasons. And now I am alone again, traveling from place to place, wandering the streets, bruised by desire, searching always for my Nikki, frantically awaiting her return."

Now he looks like he will weep. Colette says something to try to comfort him. I remain silent. I don't know what to say.

Colette stands up to go to the bathroom, and I watch her walk away, smitten. I look back at our friend. "My name's Lavender," I say. "Augustus S. Lavender."

He looks at me curiously, as though he knows that this is not my real name, that this is a code name Colette and I use in situations in which an alias is needed or useful. Then he smiles. "And I am Javier," he says. His hand is on my knee. I don't remember him putting it there. It feels natural, soothing. "You are a very quiet man, aren't you? Your attentiveness is almost frightening, as though it is all written down in your head. As though you are observing me as you do your flowers."

I laugh, a little uncomfortably. I feel my face get hot. His hand moves, gentle as a breeze, his fingers just barely sweeping my inner thigh, like a mild shock through my linen pants. "You needn't worry," I say. "I only study flowers that are fading away."

Colette returns, gives us both appraising looks, like a parent assuring herself that the two children got along okay in her absence. Under the table I move my hand into the slit in her long black skirt and run my hand up her thigh, stopping at her new tattoo, my fingers feeling the subtle relief. I can feel the warmth of her sex on my hand, but I hold back. I trace the letters with my fingers.

"This is Javier," I say, knowing now that introductions are not necessary. "Javier, this is my wife, Colette."

The man smiles and says nothing. He stands up, walks to the bar, pays his tab and ours.

I try to think of something to say to Colette. No words.

Javier returns to the table. "I thought we could continue this conversation at my place," he says. "I have a bottle of very interesting wine I'd like to drink, and I think you two could appreciate it."

Colette looks at me. Yes. I say with my eyes. Yes.

The dusk sky is the color of lilacs, smeared with pink. Javier guides us up one narrow street, down another, seemingly looping back to the first street, as if he's trying to disorient us. I surrender myself to the ecstasy of loss, of being lost, and watch Colette do the same. We swim upstream in rivers of warm air redolent with the odor of the sea and the city. We pass through the Bangladeshi neighborhood, gawking at the wholesale clothing shops and the indecipherable signs. We zig-zag through the market hall, inhaling the odor of fish and lamb, and ogling the skinless half-goats hanging from hooks, eyeballs exposed and staring off at nothing. Booksellers selling Plato and Aristotle. Dreadlocked anarchists guzzling big bottles of beer around a fire built in the sidewalk. Cops standing on the edge of Exarchos, forbidden to venture within.

We finally reach an apartment building, and Javier is quick enough to open the door and shepherd us inside that I don't get a look at the building's facade, nor do I even know which part of the city it's in. We walk up to the sixth floor, and enter the apartment. When we enter the old door, Javier does not turn on the light. The city's light – dappled by the huge, rippled windows and spilling across white walls – is enough. He beckons for us to sit in the white couch, which looks out over the city. There is music – maybe Mozart, maybe the Requiem. Javier disappears into the kitchen. Colette reaches over and kisses me, then looks me in the eyes. I look back. We both understand.

Javier emerges from the kitchen, deftly carrying a platter in one hand, a bottle and three glasses in the other. Somehow, he is able to gracefully maneuver so that he is sitting between the two of us on the couch. On the platter before us are fresh figs, pistachios, and pomegranate seeds, released from their shell. The wine bottle is odd looking, and dusty. The words on the label are written in a strange language. Javier opens it. This wine, he tells us, comes from an isolated old Jewish village in the north of Morocco. The vines are centuries old, a variety that grows only in this one valley. It is not exported; he could have been arrested for smuggling this bottle out, he says.

He pours it. We talk more about France and Greece and Italy and the way love seems to get tangled up in the light as it shimmers off the Mediterranean. We drink. We are silent. The wine infuses us with warmth. I feel as if the world no longer exists. As if this room and these high ceilings are all there is. My body feels loose. There is no judgment here. There is no reason. And words are soft.

Now, the night is in control.

Javier turns to me, looks me in the eyes. He brushes the back of his fingers against my neck.

"Your wife has beautiful lips, you know," he says.

"Yes," I reply. "Yes, she does."

"May I kiss her? Would you mind?"

"Yes," I say. I am trembling now. "You may."

And he does. They kiss gently on the couch beside me, their hands not sure where to go at first. Then his hand slips into that slit in her skirt. Shyly, her hand eventually finds his sex, rubbing gently through the thin material of his pants. My belly is burning. I take another sip of the wine. I fall back into the couch. I feel as if my sex will burst. I touch myself.

Then they stop kissing. He pulls back a bit. Still looking into her eyes, he says: "Your husband's lips are also quite beautiful. May I kiss him?"

She is a bit taken aback. Then recovers. "Of course."

He turns toward me again, and I feel as if I am floating. He is looking at me with a peaceful hunger; he desires me, in the same way that I desire Colette. I have not been on this side of desire in a long, long time, if ever. His lips touch mine. I close my eyes and concentrate on his lips and on the kiss and nothing else. His lips are soft like a woman's, his tongue warm. His hands aren't shy. He slips one underneath my shirt and touches my side below my ribs where the skin is soft. I don't know where to put my hands, so I just let one rest on his knee, the other on the back of the couch. I allow images of what will happen next flood my mind: We will take off our clothes, our bodies will mingle into one, he will bury himself in her, while my tongue pounds against her. Her orgasm will shudder through her like a wind through a forest.

I reach my hand for his thigh. I want to feel him. I want to feel his naked belly as it will feel as it moves against Colette's ass; I want to feel his throbbing sex as it will feel deep inside her; I want to feel his soft hands as they will feel, gripping her breasts so ardently as to leave bruises.

I open my eyes and see Colette looking at us. Her eyes are sleepy with lust.

Javier stops kissing me then. He sits up, pours us all another glass of that mysterious wine. Urges us both, in a hoarse voice now, to eat from the platter. We are all trembling, I am sure. And I wonder if we'll vibrate enough that our bodies, together, will create waves of sound, a chant that will linger over the rooftops, mingling with the swallows diving through the Greek sky.

"We have been watching you," Javier says, his hand on my knee, his voice less soft now. Colette has sidled up closer to us, and is looking at me, as well. It feels like a hallucination, this odd shift of mood and tone.

"We?"

"My associates and I. We are part of a non-governmental organization that brings parties together to effect change across the globe. We are intrigued by your work. We would like to help you realize your objectives."

"What does that mean?" The desire is finally ebbing from my engorged sex, but I can't help but stare at Javier's lips as he speaks, can't help but puzzle at how our freight train of lust was thrown off its tracks. "My objectives?"

"I believe you met Mr. Ivanov at the conference in Sofia."

"Yes, the oil man. The oligarch. I can't say I liked him much, nor those he surrounded himself with."

"No one expects you to be friends with the man, or to accompany him, as they say in Sofia, to the Mafia Bar. Mr. Ivanov is interested in business, and only business. He is prepared not only to fund your projects, but to make sure you and Colette are taken care of. You can live wherever you'd like."

"And what does he want from me?"

"Redemption, perhaps?"

"I'm not sure I can offer that."

"Occasionally you may be asked to do a small favor for the organization."

"Such as?"

"Nothing too burdensome, I assure you. There's no need to worry about that. The fact is, Ivanov's goals align with your own in so many ways that you'll never even know that you're working for him. Everything you do will be for the flowers. The plants."

Colette is reclined on the couch, sipping her wine, watching me intently. I look at her. We make eye contact. I am suddenly very, very scared. "And if I choose not to be part of your … organization?"

"I am afraid that's not a choice."

"Darling," Colette says, placing her hand on top of Javier's hand, which is still resting on my knee. "It will be good for you. For us. For everyone. I promise. We have the resources not only to fund your project, but also *my* projects. Finally, someone with real muscle will tackle global inequality…"

"What are you saying?!" I jump up from the couch so quickly that spots form before my eyes. "What's going on here? Colette? What… do you know Javier? Is your name even Javier? What is this … organization? What do you mean by 'we.'"

Colette stands, approaches me, runs her hand through my hair. "You need to trust us. I will explain everything in due time. But this is not the place. Surely you suspected that I… How did you think I got out of that Mafia Bar alive the other night?"

"I… I don't know. I just thought…" I fall back onto the couch. Colette fills my glass and hands it to me. She picks up one of the figs and takes a bite. In spite of it all, I feel myself getting hard again. "When you say my projects will be funded? Do you mean the…?"

"Yes, *that* project. Operation SNOW will be realized. I can assure you of that. We've already begun assembling your team."

"Team?"

"Botanists, climatologists, biologists, economists, engineers, artists, writers, journalists, physicists. It is a global operation, and will have a global reach. I believe you know Mary Aitken?"

"Yes, of course. We collaborated on a paper just last year, she…"

"She has already begun working for us. She is in the early stages of setting up an experimental station — a sort of open-air laboratory."

"Laboratory?"

"Figuratively speaking. It's in the mountains surrounding a remote Colorado town."

I take another sip of wine, aerating it on my tongue, bringing out the layers of flavor. I sit back, a warm glow spreading through my limbs. Perhaps I'm in shock. I *am* in shock. But I'm also elated. I have dreamed of this, or something like it, since I was a child: The unfettering of my creative urge, the ability to build a new world, to save countless species, to acquire the potency of a god. I look at Colette and back at Javier. Then I lift my glass. "To Operation SNOW, I guess. You don't happen to have another bottle of this, do you?"

Javier stands and smiles, walks into the other room and returns with two more bottles, popping the corks on both. "Now, perhaps we can put business aside for the rest of the evening. Shall we go to the roof, perhaps pick up where we left off?"

We follow him down the hall, walk through a door — I have to duck to fit through it — and up a narrow flight of stairs to the roof. Bats and starlings, swallows and nighthawks dart across the sky. I'm gulping the wine down now, trying to drown the anxiety, to erase what is left of inhibition.

Javier takes my empty glass and sets it on the ground. Then he is kissing me again, fervently, his hands pulling me toward him, his hard sex pressed against mine. Our clothes fall away. The clattering murmur of the city. Javier nibbles my nipple. Colette's mouth is on my mouth. The caress of the warm breeze off the sea. Hands and lips everywhere. Javier tastes like mushrooms and salt. Our three bodies fall to the rough surface of the roof and we are tangled into one.

7

December 31, 2020

The fine people of Silverton, Colorado, are overflowing with bounty when it comes to ending this rather checkered year, for tonight there will be not just one big New Year's Eve party, but two: One at the Grand Central Hotel, the other at the Antoine, a seedy bar that reputedly was frequented by French miners back in the early twentieth century, when it was nicknamed "The Frog." The former, surely, will begin as a formal affair, with people dressed in their god-awful "Victorian" attire, sipping champagne and eating chocolate-dipped strawberries before succumbing to sloppy drunkenness and not-so-covert groping on the dance floor as the midnight hour approaches. The latter, on the other hand, will hold no such pretensions, and is forecast to be a debauched Bacchanalia from beginning until the bitter end, when the notorious walk-in cooler will surely writhe with flesh and lust, and the taxidermic animal parts that adorn every wall will have been violated, vomited upon, or both. I settle on the Antoine, in part because it promises to be far more enjoyable, but also because the Grand Central permanently eighty-sixed me after that Halloween debacle a few years ago that involved a potato gun, marshmallow fluff, and a botched, backroom hand-job.

But first I have to put this week's edition of the *Dandelion Times* to bed. I was once the editor, owner, reporter, and trash-can dumper for the sole newspaper serving this mountain-bound town of five hundred or so people; now I'm back, running it for the winter while publisher Matt Jaramillo takes a well-deserved break. Back when I was in charge, I'd scramble and produce two issues before Christmas so that my lover Eliza and I could take off for the week between the two holidays. But now? Fuck it. Eliza's long gone, and my marriage to Melissa went down like the Hindenburg a few years back. I've got nowhere to go. No one to cuddle up by the fire and open presents with. No one to cook a fabulous meal for. No one. So I figured I'd stick around. Which is a good thing, because this holiday season has been anything but slow, news-wise.

It all kicked off on Christmas Day when the town tree caught fire, sending billows of black smoke into the frogbelly sky. Santa Claus was at the community dinner down at the Foreign Legion when the call came in, and being one of the few volunteer firefighters who hadn't left town for the week, he was summoned to extinguish the flames. When he got to the fire station, however, he found that his key didn't work in the locks, so he had to run back to the fire and form an honest-to-goodness bucket brigade to put it out, all the while wearing his red and white garb and his fake white beard. He was drunk, of course, so it didn't really matter. Most importantly, since I was sitting around listening to the police scanner that afternoon, I was one of the first on scene, and got great photos of the whole clusterfuck.

Sheriff Brett Conway told me that the conflagration was caused by faulty lights, and that the lock situation was the result of a misunderstanding, and that it might be best if I just didn't write about it, all things considered. But I wouldn't be silenced. I knew that this was just the latest escalation in the Great Tannenbaum War of 2020. The conflict has been raging since Thanksgiving, prompting not one, but two recall elections as well as competing boycotts of every open business in town. Now it has gone nuclear. Figuratively speaking, of course.

The day after Christmas, even as smoke still wafted from the Tannenbaum's ashes, the Runaway Cock story broke. Elly Feldengroenen, local gadfly and animal rights activist, stormed into my office and demanded that I investigate and get to the bottom of the whole kerfuffle, and to find and expose he whose cock was loose. She was clearly almost as sexually frustrated as I was, so I had empathy, and

told her to take a deep breath, slow down, and start from the beginning. When she finally calmed down she told me that she had been
snowshoeing up in Maggie's Gulch when she spied what appeared to
be a very large ptarmigan through the trees. As she crept closer she
discovered that it was, in fact, a rooster. Roosters are not endemic to
this region, obviously.

"I don't really understand what the problem is? It's just a rooster."

"You don't understand? Of course you don't. Someone dumped
that thing up there. That's cruelty to animals. And that happens to be
a blue miner rooster, a breed used in cockfighting, meaning it poses a
danger to wildlife and to skiers and other backcountry users like me.
And besides, it was really close to the abandoned Maggie May mine,
which is warm, and wet, and inviting to a cock like that. And we all
know about the Maggie May mine."

"Uhhh, we do?"

"The Atomic Energy Commission used it as a radioactive waste
dump, you idiot. What happens when a vicious rooster drinks radioactive water?"

"What?"

"You end up with an Atomic Cock, that's what."

I looked at her, not knowing what to say. How the hell had she
found out the name of my porn-star superhero? "But that's just a
conspiracy ..." I cut myself off there. "Okay, okay, I will look into it.
Have you reported it to the sheriff, yet?"

"Hell no. He's in on the whole thing."

"In on it? Oh. So, who am I supposed to interview? Who deals
with runaway poultry?"

"You could start with the only person in town who has chickens."

So after Elly left I trudged through the snow to Stan Starner's
house. He looked terrible — his face was gouged with deep scratches,
some of which seemed to be getting infected. And I won't even get
into the mullet he was sporting. "Hey, Stan, I was just wondering if
you knew anything about a rooster on the loose up Maggie Gulch-
way."

"Nope." Chickens clucked happily in the background. My translator app was on the fritz, so I can't say for certain, but I believe the

hens were rejoicing about having rid their coop of that lecherous old son-of-hen.

"Hey, what happened to your face, dude?"

"Uhhh, that? Linotype accident."

"Ouch. Well, so, um, Elly Feldengroenen's on the warpath about your cock. I mean, someone's cock. And you're the only guy with chickens so ..."

"No comment," he said, and slammed the door. I took Elly's photo of the rooster and put it on the front page. I wrestled with possible headlines: "Critics cry fowl over cock controversy." No. "Feldengroenen and Starner row over rooster." Nah. I finally settled on: "WANTED DEAD OR ALIVE: Fugitive Cock." In the end I elected to leave Stan's name out of it. He and Elly had some history; Elly and just about everyone had some history — myself included, if you count that night in Antoine's walk-in cooler with the whipped cream, the frozen beef patties, and the American cheese singles, which, in the heat of the moment, I mistook for prophylactic devices. And I figure maybe she ginned the whole thing up in order to get revenge or something, and didn't want to put myself in the path of a libel lawsuit. Elly won't like my coverage, but then she wasn't so keen on the cheese slices, either.

As if that weren't news enough to fill an eight-page paper, on the penultimate day of the year Leather Fred's latest calendar dropped. Leather Fred is one of those Silverton characters who came from somewhere else, but no one knows where, or when, or even how old he is. He's like the rest of us, in other words, and he's been around long enough to become a fixture, like Wolfie the dog or The Christ of the Mines statue overlooking town. I'm not saying that Leather Fred is Jesus, necessarily, but he does have a similar aura. His monicker comes from the only material he will put next to his skin. His shoes are leather, his hat is leather, his pants are leather, and, yes, his underwear is leather, to which I, unfortunately, can attest.

Leather Fred is the dump tender. There's no trash service in Silverton, so we all have to haul our own garbage or recyclables or coal clinkers up to the transfer station, and Leather Fred is the guy who keeps us all in line. His work uniform is the same in December as it is in May: leather chaps, a leather hat, leather steel-toed work boots, a leather choker, and a leather g-string. That's it. He likes to talk to folks as they dump their trash, sometimes for hours. I can handle that; I've got nothing better to do. But he also insists on hugging everyone who visits. I'm not a hugging kind of guy, particularly when the one doing the hugging is wearing leather chaps and a g-string and not much else. As a result, I have been known to let six months or more worth of garbage pile up in the shed out back. Yes, I am aware that I have issues, thank you very much. But try getting therapy or any emotional support at all in this place, a place where AA meetings tend to be held at the Miner's Tavern, and the sex addicts support group takes place in the aforementioned walk-in cooler at Antoine's, whipped cream canisters included. Or so I've heard.

The newsworthy thing is the calendar, which has six pictures of men and six pictures of women wearing, yes, leather. In the early days Fred photocopied the whole thing in the library, and handed it out for free to his friends. You could barely even make out what or who was in the photos, and it was in no way offensive except to vegans. But ever since he got banned from the library copy machine he has really upped his calendar-producing game, and now he sells the thing for fifteen bucks a pop. People pay because the models wear fewer and fewer items of clothing with each passing year. This year Fred's kicked things up about a million notches. Not only are the models scantily clad, but also they are all performing sex acts with one another — women on men, men on men, women on women, you name it. February is for S&M, May for masturbation, and December is an all out orgy scene. The models are all wearing masks or otherwise have their faces obscured, but those of us who have visited the aforementioned walk-in cooler on a Friday night in mud season recognize some of the other body parts. In other words, this is a purely homegrown operation, which has not only caused the calendars to sell out in just hours, tripling the county GDP, but has also thrown the more repressed sectors of the populace into a bit of a tizzy, giving me yet more fodder for the front page. It turns out that a scandal over a bunch of loose cocks will overshadow a single runaway rooster any day, much to Elly Feldengroenen's dismay.

I wrap it all up and send the last paper of the year off to the printer, lock up the office, and go on a long kicksled on the icy streets of

Silverton. That's how we get around in Silverton in the winter time, some of us, anyway. The sleds look like dogsleds, only smaller. You stand on one of the runners with one foot and kick with the other and glide along the hard packed snow. The air is weirdly warm — relatively speaking — and moist, the clouds low and thick and obscuring the upper slopes of Kendall, Sultan, Boulder, Anvil, and King Solomon, a few of the peaks that ring our little town. It seems like as good a day to die as any other, so I start kicking up Quality Hill for a sled run down Tenth Street. But then I remember what happened to Jonny Thompson and I think better of it, and head over to the Battleship for some caffeine, instead. The windows are all steamed up from within, and when I open the door I'm blasted by warmth and the bustle of the crowd. It's the usual clientele, fortified by a whopping dose of skiers from the lowlands wanting first dibs on New Year's Day powder, all of whom fit the mountain town archetype: Well-worn Carhartts and a duct-taped down Patagonia jacket, scruff, fashionably dirty hair, and eyes and skin and liver showing the effects of too much sun, wind, and micro-distilled booze.

I walk up to the bar, where Olivia Patel, the establishment's owner, is flinging shots at breakneck speed. Everything on the menu is named after avalanche paths, or snow types, or other geologic hazards. You can get a Riverside sandwich, an Irene pizza, Graupel (a form of snow, or oatmeal), or, the strongest coffee drink known to man or woman, and my usual choice: "I'll have a depth hoar, Olivia. Make it a triple."

You fucking misogynistic pig," she screams back at me, wielding the still-steaming portafilter like a hammer, used espresso grounds spattering my face. "How dare you use a word like that in my establishment! Out!" All the newcomers or out-of-towners in the coffee shop stop talking and stare at me, including Erin, the new woman in town whom I've been mustering up the courage to ask out on a date. The locals don't care. Olivia pulls the same act every time I order. You'd think by now it would get old.

"Just kidding, Malcolm," Olivia says, far too quietly for anyone to hear. "One depth hoar coming up." Depth hoar is what happens when it snows a lot in October and November and then stops during the typical December dry spell. The freeze-thaw cycle rots the snow so you get a bunch of faceted snow crystals that can't bond with one another. Add another big dump of snow on top of that, and you've got the recipe for an avalanche disaster. Right now we've got a good six feet of rotten ass snow sitting on the slopes thanks to record-breaking snowfall in October and November. Now a big storm is on its way.

I grab my drink and head to the only person I see who I know who will still talk to me after Olivia's rant: Robert Jensen, practitioner of zen-redneck snow science and avalanche forecasting. "Well, well, if it isn't the yellow journalist, himself," Jensen says. "I got a story for you: There's a moisture-laden San Juaner coming off the Pacific and it's gonna fuck us right up the ass, starting tonight. It's already dumping snow over on Lizard Head. If I weren't so stupid I'd get the fuck out of this place right now. Because after tonight there will be no getting out for days. You know what that means, don't you?"

"No. What?"

"The milk runs out first, then the booze, then the cigarettes. After that, there's nothing to do but throw a community orgy in the school gym, led by Leather Fred."

With this less-than-savory image freeze-framed on my mental movie screen, I head back to my apartment, take a coffee nap, make some dinner, check out Eliza's social media pages to see what she's up to, realize how stupid that is, consider sexting Melissa, reconsider, unfollow Eliza, refollow Eliza, stalk Melissa's social media — she's apparently working at a greenhouse for some dreamboat -- slam the laptop shut with jealousy, take another nap, and then head down to Antoine's. I am worried about being too early, about standing around awkwardly with the three other nerds that will show up on time, try-ing to make small talk about the weather: "So, I hear a big storm's on its way." "Yeah, a big one. Might even be a San Juaner." "Yeah, I bet it snows a lot." "Nothing like seventy-six. There will never be a win-ter like that." And so on. But no. This party is already raging, and judging by the generally loose behavior of the crowd, most folks are at least three drinks in. After briefly worrying that I may have missed out on something, I plow through the crowd to the bar where not one, but three bartenders are mixing drinks. I make a beeline for Sandy, the Australian dozer-driver-turned-bartender.

"What'll ya have?"

"Well, if it's not too much trouble, a Manhattan." I immediately regret the choice. Too elitist — Sandy probably will have to look it up in her cocktail recipe book or something; too patriarchal — Eliza would surely burn me alive if she caught me imbibing something straight out of Mad Men. What can a guy drink these days without making some sort of social, class, or political statement? A margarita? Oh, no, cultural appropriation. Fuck it.

"It ain't too much trouble for you, honey. Sweet or dry vermouth?"

"Wow. Dry, with a cherry."

"No."

"No?"

"You can't drink a *dry* Manhattan with a cherry. What kind of philistine are you, anyway? A twist it is."

There are a few very brief recurring moments in life that are perfect, that I'd like to freeze and just hold there, and one of them is when Sandy the dozer-driver calls me a philistine, another is that first sip of a finely mixed cocktail, particularly a Manhattan — the cold, the burn, the smoky sweetness. If only I could just leave it there I'd be a much better person, I'm sure. Instead, I keep taking sips, hoping to relive the first sip of the night and always failing. I watch the crowd. It feels good, the first-drink-of-the-night-buzz, the crowd of people, some of them friends, some acquaintances, and all of them familiar somehow. It's like old times. Maybe it is old times. I wish Eliza were here to play the Bar Game with me. Eliza is not here.

Kate Greenwell and Ingmar Nelson come to the bar and say hello. I ask Nelson, the local ski area safety director, if the area will be open tomorrow. Nelson rolls his eyes, seems agitated. "Mears seems to think so. I'm not so sure. We're gonna have to get up there and bomb the shit out of the place in order to make it safe, and we can't fly with bad visibility, so all these hungover powder hounds here will end up scouring the hillsides looking for freshies. I predict that someone will die. I heard CDOT already closed Red due to visibility, and the Blue Point's down, too."

"If they close South then the highway· crew won't have to work anymore, and they can come over and party with us. I owe Robert Jensen a Pisco or five."

"Good for them. Unfortunately I have to work either way."

The couple, their arms intertwined, drift away to order more drinks. I finish mine, resist ordering another, for now, and meander slowly through the crowd, looking for familiar faces, hoping to find Erin, the new woman in town. Leather Fred is on a little stage moving some sound equipment around, presumably for the local cover band to play. Fred, naturally, is wearing shiny leather pants, a leather shirt, a leather jacket, and a spiked leather dog collar. Saying hello to Fred could end up being a several-hour-long affair, so I veer off in the opposite direction. I feel a hearty slap on my back.

"Brautigan! You're here! I've been looking for you, man."

"Ha, ha, if it ain't Charlie Simpson. Or should I call you Judge Simpson, esquire."

"You can call me whatever you want, man, but you can't buy me a drink."

"You're the county judge. Brett's the sheriff. What's next? Fred's gonna be mayor?"

"Holy shit, that would be something, now, wouldn't it? Hey, man, now that you're back I just wanna make sure you're not gonna write about, well, you know…"

I search my brain for dirt I might have on Simpson. There was that time we drank too much tequila and vomited off the roof of the Grand Central on a group of tourists dressed in Victorian garb, but hey, that type of behavior is a credibility-builder in these parts, not blackmail material.

"You know, man," he whispers out of the side of his mouth. "The thing about a certain Latin American revolutionary's head?"

"Oh, shit, yeah, yeah, no, no, I would never…"

"Oh, good, good, I just wanted to make sure. Hey, I gotta go talk to Michelle about some business. Let me buy you a drink later, okay?"

"Sure thing."

I stare into space, trying to understand the passage of time, and the way people change — and don't change — over the years. Neil Olsen's sitting at a table, a glass of water in his hand, looking into the blur of bodies and listening into the blur of voices. Maybe he's dreaming of his days working underground, or the time he and Bud took drunken flight off of the Champion Cliffs in a 1969 Ford Fair-line, and lived to drink many more bottles of Old Crow. Mike Mason, clearly three sheets to the wind, is ranting drunkenly to a young couple that can't keep their hands off of one another. I duck back into the crowd. If Mason sees me he will, once again, try to coax me into signing up for the local volunteer fire department. I might do it if I thought it would help me get laid, but it's more likely to get me cast as Santa Claus next Christmas.

I'm shaken out of my reverie by the feeling of a hand on my ass. I move subtly away from the hand, but it persists. And then it squeezes my buttock. I turn around and do a little backwards skip as I find myself looking down into the face of Mary Aitken, all five-feet-three of her, looking even more beautiful than she did fourteen years ago when she fled my office after planting a very memorable kiss on my lips.

"You look like a deer in the headlights, Malcolm. Do I really scare you that much?"

"No, I'm not scared. What makes you say that?" I look around the crowd for her husband. Was it David? "It's just a little noisy, that's all."

"I've been divorced for years," she says.

"Oh. Oh, good. I mean. I'm sorry. Me too. I mean, I got married. Not to Eliza, to Melissa. But we're no longer... We split up a while back. Hey, can I buy you a drink?"

Sandy gives Mary the once-over then hands her a gin and tonic — a colonial cocktail if I ever saw one — and another Manhattan to me, giving a subtle eyebrow rise as she does so. We take our drinks to a corner table where the light is dim and the jarring sound from the first band, Mongolian Dust Storm, is slightly less overpowering.

Mary is still her same vivacious self, her somewhat bubbly de-meanor belying the intensity of her intellect. She still has her big smile, her long, shiny wheat- and honey-hued hair, and she still can talk in a way that I find both endearing and soothing. We talk a lot, about the last several years, about our ruined relationships, about how it feels to be alone after so many years of sharing a bed and a life. Mary says a lot, but at the same time seems oddly reserved, as if she has a lot more to say, but can't, or won't, or is waiting for a more opportune time. I want to ask her about that night so many years ago, the night of the kiss, and the phone call, and the fact that she just vanished after that. Where did she go?

"Are you checking out my cleavage?"

"What?! Oh. No, no, I was…"

"It's okay if you are."

"No, well, maybe a little bit, ha ha. But actually I was looking at the freckle on your chest. That one." I point, longing to touch, but refraining.

"And? Are you a dermatologist now or something?"

Now that I'm this deep in the hole, with almost two strong drinks down, I figure I might as well be honest. "I once wrote a poem about that mole. About how I wanted to kiss it. How I wanted to draw a dot-to-dot picture on your body with my lips and my tongue. It was a terrible poem. I deleted if off my computer after… well, you know."

Mary Aitken says nothing, is silent for the first time that night. Fuck, I've finally done it, haven't I? I've gone too far. Tomorrow morning I'll wake up and find myself on one of those #MeToo lists. "I'm sorry. That was not cool to say that. Or to look at your mole. I'm so sorry. I'm such an ass. I'm a little tipsy."

"Yes, you are an ass. But not for staring at my breasts. For not giving me that poem. Why?"

"It was awful, for one thing, too cheesy and sentimental and… Hey. Your drink's empty. Let me get you another."

She is smiling now, the lines around her eyes the sexiest thing I have ever beheld.

"You think that bartender knows how to make a martini?"

"Oh, you bet she does."

Too Little O2 takes the stage and starts ripping out corny cover songs and Mary gets up to dance, so I follow. She's obviously intent on turning it into her daily cardio workout, gyrating and undulating and thrusting and parrying in ways that defy anatomical laws. I try my best to keep up, managing only to become a sweat-soaked mess. Mary's face, strong shoulders, and arms are covered with a glistening sheen. During a break between songs, Mary finally leads me back to her table. She looks at her watch."

"It's eleven-thirty," she says, finishing off her martini. "I can think of several ways I'd rather ring in the New Year than with a bunch of drunk Silverton folks."

"Oh. Okay. Ummm, well, it was super nice hanging out with you. And great to see you…"

"You really are obtuse, aren't you?"

"Huh?"

"Put your coat on. Put your hat on. Put your gloves on. Settle up our bar tab. And meet me outside. You're giving me a ride home on that sled of yours. And just in case you're wondering, that would be your place that we are going to. Together. Got it?"

About ten inches of fresh powder covers the street when I stumble out into the cold. The snow's still coming down, the wind blowing, too. Voices. Under an old awning, Nelson, the snow safety guy, and Bobby Mears, the ski area owner, are huddled together, talking intensely. I try to eavesdrop — it's my job, after all — but only hear the tone of their voices, not the actual words.

"Wow. This is a real San Juaner," I say. The two men look startled to see me. "What, two or three inches an hour? More?"

"Hey, Malcolm," Nelson says.

"I'll see you tomorrow," Mears says to Nelson. Then, looking at me with a sneer: "Happy New Year." He stomps into the darkness.

"Geez. What's with him?"

Nelson says nothing, just looks out into the darkness and then skyward, so that the big flakes fall on his face and into his open mouth. Then he turns to me. "I guess it's working."

"Huh?"

"The cloud seeding operation. Some new technology. You know those two guys who have been hanging around? The ones with the Porsche?"

"Yeah," I say. I had noticed them. Who wouldn't? "I've seen them around. Who are they?"

"They're assholes, that's who they are. And Mears is getting tangled up in …"

"In what?"

"Nothing. I shouldn't be telling you this. Forget I said anything. Please. I'll catch you around." He goes back inside. A moment later Mary comes out. She bends down and scoops up some snow. "Quite a bit of moisture. I bet some good slides are running already."

We both look south, in the direction of the highway into town, to see if any lights appear — an indication that the road has not yet closed. But the road is closed.

"Way too much fresh to sled, I'm afraid."

Mary sits down on the sled's seat, anyway. "Too bad. If you wanna get a girl home, you gotta do the work."

So I do. It's more of a slog than a sled, taking a good ten minutes to go three blocks. As I approach my apartment, I try to map out what will transpire once we reach the apartment. I'll offer Mary a drink, maybe some food. We can, what, watch television? See the ball drop? Then what? The possibilities are enough to make my legs feel like they're filled with jelly.

"Well, that took a while. You live up there?"

"Yep. For now. I'm housesitting."

"That stairway is a friggin' hazard. Those icicles are serious. And look at that wind slab forming off the roof. You should probably wear a beacon whenever you go outside. Okay. You first."

We climb the stairs as quickly and gingerly as we can given all the snow, and stomp our feet off before stepping inside. I have one shoe off when I feel Mary's arms on my chest, pushing me against the wall as if she's trying to get me out of harm's way, but that's not it at all. She is shoving me in front of a freight train, a freight train of desire. She kisses me frantically on the mouth, her hands back down to my belt as if picking up where we left off ten months earlier. Clothes come off in stages. A jacket here, pants there, a sock, a bra, underwear. Fingernails and sweat. Clenched fist and salt. Hunger, hunger, hunger, hunger. We stumble toward the bedroom and into a universe of hair and lips, slippery and smooth, teeth and spit, flesh and bone. And when the courthouse clock chimes midnight, I find myself nestled between Mary Aitken's warm and creamy thighs, her hips levitating frantically to meet the insistent rhythm of my tongue.

"Happy New Years." I open my eyes. Mary is propped up on an elbow, looking at me impatiently. "It's about time you woke up. I've been waiting…" The view out the window next to the bed is all white. Snow is piled on the narrow window sill, little crystalline flakes cling to the outside of the glass, and it continues to fall. Mary's fingers are running up and down my sternum, twirling up tufts of chest hair and pulling, gently.

"Say something," she says, after a minute or two of silence.

"Wow."

"That's profound."

"It was that, too. Holy wow. That was… Wow."

"I'm flattered. You have quite the athletic tongue, yourself. Now, quit uttering nonsense and tell me about that poem you wrote about my mole."

"It's a freckle, isn't it? It's silly."

"I don't care."

"I can't remember it."

"Sure you can."

I roll over, propping myself up on my elbow, too, so we are facing each other. I touch the freckle-mole, and move my finger slowly to another on her chest. "Let's just say that I rhymed clavicle with magical, and hotty with spotty and body." My fingers continue to draw on her flesh, following the contours of her curves. She half closes her eyes. I slide the down comforter away from her torso. "And I compared your body to a star map." I switch drawing tools, from finger to tongue. She utters a soft coo from deep in her throat. I navigate her galaxy, lingering in the places that count, her hands in my hair, pressing me to her.

Her generous lips curl back on her teeth when she comes.

Later: "What's up with that tattoo on your thigh?" I ask. "Looks Russian. You're not a secret agent are you?"

"It says snyag. Means snow. In Bulgarian."

"Bulgarian?"

"Yeah."

"Huh? Hey, Mary, umm, what happened last time? You just disappeared without ever saying goodbye or anything. And now… Why are you here?"

"To screw you. That's not obvious?"

"No, I mean, why are you in Silverton? Last night Ingmar Nelson mentioned something about cloud seeding. Do you have something to do with that? The project you were working on?"

She looks away, mumbles something.

"Excuse me?"

"You need to be careful… " She's about to say more but is cut off by a loud, staticky voice coming from the kitchen: The police scanner. I brought it home to keep me company during the long nights. The sheriff's dispatcher is saying something about an avalanche, about victims, multiple victims.

"Holy shit," I say, jumping up and throwing on my pants. "Someone's buried. I gotta go, Mary. Come with?"

"I'll wait here, if that's okay with you."

"Sure, of course. I won't be long. I just gotta check it out. You know, my job."

Incident command, if you can call it that, is a cluster of CDOT trucks, sheriff department vehicles, and the search and rescue suburban in the parking lot of the gas station at the edge of town. Everyone's lethargic and hungover, but also antsy and somewhat confused. An anonymous report came in that morning of up to four people buried in the North Battleship snow slide. But it's far too dangerous for the rescuers to even begin to approach the scene until the route is cleared with explosives. But the slide shooting crew is trapped halfway between Silverton and Durango. I wait around with everyone for several hours, trying to get material for a story. Finally, as the day begins to take on the deep blue of a stormy winter late afternoon, I head back home, climbing up the treacherous stairs to the apartment.

I know she's gone. I call out her name when I open the door anyway. I walk through the apartment. The bed is made. The kitchen is clean. She hasn't left a note. We never exchanged phone numbers. I begin to wonder if the night before wasn't a dream, if Mary Aitken isn't some sort of specter. Outside the storm is raging again, snow piling up rapidly, erasing the work that the snowplows had done just moments before. I pour myself a Scotch, sit down in the chair looking out over Silverton's main drag. Darkness comes. The streetlights flicker on, and snowflakes flutter in their glow like moths swarming to the flame. I turn on some Nina Simone, my go-to in situations like this. I sip slowly, waiting, just waiting.

The streetlights flicker out, as do the lights in the windows across the street from mine. Nina is silenced. The omnipresent humming of electrical machines ceases. I look at my phone; it still has its reassuring glow, but there is no signal. The voices on the police scanner have gone mute.

It's alright, I tell myself, over and over again:: The snow will stop, the roads will open, the power will come back on, the avalanche victims will wander out unharmed, and pretty soon I'll hear the footsteps of Mary Aitken climbing the back stairs, the creak of the door as she enters the apartment, the soft padding of her bare feet walking across the floor, and her whispered words as she envelops my body in hers. I believe none of it.

8

February 2020

"What the fuck is up with the weather?" Melissa asked no one as she climbed out of her car on the fourth and purportedly last day of August's sojourn. "I think we could all use a little bit of that global warming." It was February fourteenth. That it was also Valentines Day signified less to Melissa than the fact that in any other year over the last decade or so winter would be waning by now, crocuses would be poking their way through the cold dirt along south-facing walls, the red switches of pussy-willows would be topped with tight buds, the light would take on a different quality, the snow would melt in the lowlands, and the earth would turn into shoe-stealing muck.

But this year something had gone haywire. Winter had come in with unusual intensity in November and now, like that dude you knew in high school who wanted to crash on your couch for "a few days," refused to leave. The sky was perpetually gray, the air perpet-

74

ually cold, and snow was still piling up relentlessly in the high country. Apparently Silverton, up in Colorado, the town where she and Malcolm had gotten together and a place she'd prefer to forget, had been blockaded by avalanches for weeks. When Melissa had complained to her mother about the crazy weather, her mom had laughed: "This is what February's *supposed* to be like."

So maybe that which had gone haywire was now going back to "normal?" Melissa considered what Augustus had said before he left, about his big operation. He hadn't come out and said said he was tinkering with the weather or the climate, but it sure did sound like that. Could this be his doing? Was he trying to save the plants by freezing the hell out of all the humans? I mean, it might work, but still. "Fuck that guy if this is his doing," Melissa said as she opened the greenhouse door, letting the wet warmth wash over her. "And fuck that guy anyway." As if on cue, her phone rang out with the melody from Bruce Springsteen's "I'm on Fire," indicating that Augustus had sent her a text: "Dearest Melissa, Regretfully I must remain here in the Balkans for an additional two or more days. I hope this isn't too much of an inconvenience. I do miss you and my flowers. Faithfully yours, Augustus."

Melissa slammed the phone down on the table, clenched her fists, scrunched up her face, and let out a high pitched wail. "What the hell could keep him at some botany conference for an extra two days?" She didn't want to know, and was mad at herself for not wanting to know. Melissa Nyquist, who prided herself on her lack of jealousy, was burning with it. She pulled out the phone and started to write a "fuck you" text, but then she inhaled, felt the warm moisture in her lungs, smelled the musky, fecund aroma of life all around her, and changed her mind. "I truly do understand," she typed. "I am happy to care for the plants for as long as you need me to, and I eagerly await your return. Happy Valentines Day." She erased the last part. Too smarmy. Replaced it with, "xo, m."

She put the phone back in her pocket and, without thinking about it, unbuttoned her shirt. It felt like the tropics, so why not dress as if she were in the tropics? She took the shirt off and then her faded jeans, and worked for a bit in just a bra and underwear, cursing herself for not thinking of this earlier. As she was transplanting a basil seedling, she accidentally rubbed the root ball against her bra, leaving a brown smudge. It was her only bra, and she didn't have a washing machine at home, and going to the laundromat was a harrowing experience for any number of reasons. So, not wanting to get her bra any dirtier, she removed it. The condensation blanketed the glass walls and, anyway, no one could see over the adobe wall encircling the property. She was also wearing one of two pairs of underwear with good elastic. So she slipped them off, too, hanging them delicately on the fig tree's branch. Then, liberated from her clothing, she went about completing her daily tasks. It felt so good that she didn't want to stop, and sure as hell didn't want to leave the warm womb of the greenhouse and return to the eyeball-shattering cold. So when she finished her rounds she began again, and then again, misting leaves, aerating the soil around the trees, reciting bad poetry to the goldfish in the pools that provided thermal mass.

Finally, as the light outside faded into deep blue, with a sharp line of pink down near the western horizon, Melissa reluctantly prepared to leave. Still unclothed, she went to the little table in the middle of the greenhouse to write down her hours and her daily journal entry where she made note of anything unusual that she might have observed regarding the plants. When she picked up the journal — a Moleskine, naturally — a piece of paper fell out. Someone had written a poem of sorts on it. A Valentines Day poem. It was touching, but also odd, as if part of it were missing.

You are my pillow.
You are the splinter
under my fingernail.
You are my sparkplug.

The tone didn't seem very Augustus-like. It was too whimsical? Too light? She wasn't sure.

I don't need a special day
to peel off my skin, inch by inch
and wrap it around you ...

... your ass
as you saunter away from our bed in the morning
in your underwear

making my desire ache all the way into my bones.
I heart your upside down heart.
What the fuck? She knew this poem. And not from a book.
You are my desert.
Your belly the starfilled bowl of the sky.
Your thighs moonlit sandstone.
Your sex a dragonfly-fluttered pool
so laden with moss that I forget my way.
Blinded by hunger
I must follow the compass with my mouth
urgently
as though the secret to all things
is hidden in the depths.
And then I find it:
the parting of your lips.

I am your table.
I am your ballpoint pen.
But maybe for just this one day
you will grant my wish
and let me be
the thorn on your rose
or the dew gathering gently
on the smooth rim
of your cocktail glass.

Malcolm Brautigan, her ex-husband, had written these very same words for Melissa. She was certain of it. So how the fuck did they end up here? Was he Augustus's lover? Did he recycle the poem for him? Or maybe Malcolm had stolen the poem from the back of a Hallmark card and passed it off as his own. That was the most likely scenario. No wonder she left the asshole.

She put the poem carefully back in the notebook, wrote down her hours, and then looked around the greenhouse at the plants, trying to come up with something to write. And that's when she saw it, the Rothschild orchid, in bloom. "O M G," she muttered.

When August had first pointed the plant out Melissa was indifferent. It looked like just another plant to her. But in the days that followed she noticed that he acted differently when he was in that part of the greenhouse, walked more reverently, perhaps. So she looked it up online one night after work. Not only is it listed as endangered (and so might be contraband), but a single stem could fetch five grand or more. Apparently the things grow only in one eco-zone on the slope of one mountain in Malaysia. August had told her to steer clear of the plant altogether, but screw that. I mean, she *had* to get a look at a five-thousand-dollar flower, didn't she? Still naked, she approached the flower slowly. It had two narrow wings with zebra stripes, and what looked like two mandibles, also striped, that wanted to eat her up. In the center was a hairy plumb-like organ that made her think of a clitoris — the humidity, again, was making her horny.

She started to back off, having no intention of getting on August's bad side. Maybe he didn't yearn for her like she yearned for him, but he did give her a job, and the pay was damned good, and he was a nice guy. Still, the bloom wouldn't last forever, and maybe it would never return. It would be silly, even reckless, to refrain from getting a whiff of the most expensive flower on earth. She approached it cautiously and slowly, closed her eyes and her mouth, and inhaled deeply through her large schnoz. She wrinkled up her nose and raised an eyebrow. Hmmm. It really didn't smell like a flower at all, at least not any flower she'd ever smelled. This was no rose or lilac. It was musky, animal-like, dark, earthy. But also intoxicating — a swooning scent. Her legs felt like jelly. Her skin became hyper-sensitive, so that the warm, wet breeze emanating from the little fan on the other side of the room felt like a caress. Hunger washed over her, a carnal hunger. Her fingers brushed across her belly, the sensation sharp, as if someone else were touching her. Her fingers dropped down to her sex, wet and hot, slippery and engorged.

August sat in the dimly-lit bar, transfixed by what appeared on his telephone screen.

He should have been thrilled to make this trip to Bulgaria to meet with Ivan Ivanov in his villa on the slopes of Vitosha Mountain, overlooking Sofia. It was to be a celebration of sorts, a prelude to the final phase of Operation SNOW's implementation. Mary Aitken and her team had achieved remarkable results in the facilities above the old mining town of Silverton, Colorado and experiments in Bulgaria, Canada, Estonia, and Pakistan were similarly successful.

Just as impressive, and terrifying, was Ivanov's network's ability to keep the whole thing under wraps. There had been some touchy moments, like when the "chemtrail" videos had somehow made their way to YouTube. But that was easily brushed off as conspiracy-theory nuttiness by Ivanov's people. More worrisome was Colette's ultimately fatal crisis of conscience that led her to tip off that journalist, Brautigan. Luckily Brautigan's editor was in the fold, and quickly squelched the whole thing. Later, she was able to even bring Brautigan into the organization, without him even knowing it.

All that remained to do was to link up all the separate stations to create a planet-blanketing climate control apparatus, truly the only hope for averting a global catastrophe and mass extinction. The team's leaders would all be in Bulgaria to put the final step into motion, to culminate August's life's work. And yet, as he stepped off the plane in Sofia, he was overcome with foreboding and anxiety so severe that he ordered his driver to stop on the way to Ivanov's villa and purchase a bottle of rakia for the ride.

Ivanov was a megalomaniac, that much was always clear, and like all megalomaniacs, he was never satisfied, never could have enough power or money. As if altering the climate at will was not enough. He wanted to control governments, the media, the collective brain of all seven billion people on earth. His methods were crude, to be sure, even harebrained — or so it had once seemed. August actually laughed out loud when he learned that Ivanov and his buddy Vladimir Putin planned to install a buffoonish real estate heir into the U.S. Presidency, and he saw Ivanov's quest to influence every aspect of human thought by taking control of Facebook's algorithms as absurd. And yet, now who's laughing?

August could let all of that go, since it really didn't affect his project. But now that Operation SNOW was up and ready for implementation, Ivanov was gradually seizing control of it, to use for his own nefarious purposes — it was already in progress up in Silverton. To demonstrate, Ivanov ordered the Vitosha Mountain station to give a passing snowstorm a bit of what he crudely called "weather steroids." Nearly four feet of snow piled up in Sofia over just a few hours, putting a stranglehold on the city. And who came to the rescue? Ivanov, of course, with his fleet of snowplows, helicopters, and road crews. Sensing August's reticence, Ivanov had commanded that he stay in Bulgaria longer, that he accompany him to the Black Sea to see his yacht and his oil tankers, that he fly with him on his helicopter to North Macedonia to visit the fake news and click farms. "They are no different than your weather stations," Ivanov had said. "But they modify the collective consciousness instead of the climate."

When August saw an opening, he had fled, claiming that he was needed back in Santa Fe to continue to work with the new asset. That Ivanov had not at all resisted worried August, and invoked visions of Novichok and ricin, of the hiss-and-thud of a silenced gunshot. He would always have to watch his back, and that would never be enough. Now he was in the Frankfurt airport, using gin to dull his anxiety and preemptively to render the long flight back to Albuquerque bearable. It was as he took sip number one of martini number two that his home-alarm app started dinging on his phone.

August wasn't a home security kind of guy, even when it came to his greenhouse. He knew that if he put bars and alarms and cameras all over the place people would think that his greenhouse was full of marijuana, and they'd surely rob it. So he had a minimalist policy when it came to security — if someone wanted to steal his tomatoes, they could have them. But the Rothschild orchid was another matter. He refused to put it in a cage or behind glass; that wouldn't be fair to the plant, now, would it? So, instead, he installed a hidden network of motion sensors right around the plant that triggered an alarm on his phone and switched on the greenhouse webcam. If anyone got near the plant, they'd become phone-video stars in real time.

When the alert went off, August checked the time, and after a quick calculation realized that Melissa would have finished her day's work hours earlier. Someone was trying to pilfer the orchid. He switched on the camera monitor even as he tried to work out how to call the Santa Fe police — and what he'd say to them. But on his screen he saw no ski-masked thief running away with a delicate flower, nor did he see an empty podium where the purloined plant once stood. No, the plant was still there and, much to his surprise, in bloom. That alone confounded him enough that it took him a moment to notice she who had tripped the alarm and camera, she who was now writhing in the dirt underneath the fig tree, one hand stroking her sex furiously while the other reached up and plucked one of the wet and juicy fruits off of the tree and stuffed it into her mouth. August literally fell off his barstool — not from shock or dismay, but from desire.

Melissa woke up in the dirt, disoriented, staring at the smooth trunk of the fig tree. Light filtered through the green from outside, but when she reached into her pocket for her phone to check the time it wasn't there, namely because her pocket wasn't there because she wasn't wearing any clothes. Had she been asleep for hours, minutes, or days? She didn't know.

It was that fucking flower that did it, that had knocked her into some sort of trance of longing and lasciviousness. She remembered trying to get up to leave, but each time she was forced to stop and lean up against the tree or lay down in the dirt and bring herself to orgasm. She got hungry, so she ate the figs, their fleshy consistency further fueling her ardor. Finally her legs just gave out and she lay down and passed out.

She slowly sat up and looked around. The figs were all gone. But damn were they good. August was full of shit when he said they weren't ripe; he just wanted to hog them all to himself. The plants around her were vaguely smooshed, but it looked like they'd survive. While careening around in a lustful haze she apparently had not attempted to fuck the orchid or anything like that, because it still sat ostentatiously on its pedestal, just like before. "Slut," she muttered to the showy flower. She stood up, brushed herself off. August wasn't due back for another day, so she had plenty of time to clean things up and restore order to the greenhouse, figs excepted. She reached down and picked up her underwear, balanced on one foot while pulling them on to the other leg.

"Freeze," said the voice from behind her. It sounded like August, but with a tinge of something like desperation. "You are so, so…"

She turned around. August stood in the greenhouse doorway, staring at her with those mysterious eyes. His face was pale. He trembled.

"About the figs," she said, still standing on one foot, her underwear only halfway on. "I'm sorry. It's just that, they really seemed to be ripe, and I read that once they ripen, you have to pick them and eat them quickly or …"

"I have cameras," he said, motioning to the little boxes on the ceiling as he walked toward her slowly. "I should have told you. They come on only when someone gets close to the orchid."

"Cameras?"

"I was watching."

"Oh. I was just. I wanted a closer look. I'm sorry."

"Ssshhhh. I'm the one who should be sorry."

"You were watching? You mean….?"

"Yes, oh yes, oh yes, oh yes. It was the longest flight of my life."

And then she kissed him. Lips. Teeth. Tongues. A melody of moans. They fell to their knees. She lay back in the soft, warm dirt. His mouth was everywhere: Her earlobe, her eyelid, her clavicle, her nipple, her hip, her sex. He took her labia between his lips and sucked lightly, darting his tongue into her salty warmth. He grasped her clitoris between his teeth, massaged it with his tongue, his fingers exploring without limits, pushing all of her buttons at once. She circled her hips slowly around, uttering deep moans and squeezing her breasts. His intensity increased, and so did hers, her face and chest blooming scarlet. Then she cried out, her hips thrusting into his face until the orgasm hit — quick and sharp like an electrical shock rippling up through her belly. She pushed him away, but he would not relent, and she fell into his rhythm again. The second orgasm was fuller, softer. And the third felt like a sweet and syrupy cluster bomb had detonated somewhere deep inside her, spreading one wave of pleasure after another all the way up to the space behind her eyeballs.

 Then she saw the tomato. Deep yellow, it seemed to glow from within, and pulled the vine over with its ripe weight. At least five or six hung from the one plant; dozens more begged lusciously to be eaten from surrounding vines. Melissa smiled mischievously, reached over and picked the ripest looking one. It burst sweetly and tartly in her mouth, the juice squirting onto her lips – a flavor like no other, sunshine on the tongue. She lifted the remainder to August's lips. He took a bite then kissed her, letting the slippery little seeds slip from his tongue onto hers.

She pushed him onto his back, plucked another tomato all heavy from the vine, and knelt down before him as if in prayer. She delicately touched his sex, long and thick, hard and throbbing, the skin fragile and silky like the petal of a rose. She ran her tongue along the veins lightly. Then she held the tomato over his phallus and burst the fruit so that the tart juice slathered his sex. He shuddered almost violently as she took him in her mouth, all of him, and when he came he let out a guttural cry that seemed as if it came from deep down in the roots of the plants. They did it again, and again, until finally, when the purple sky of dusk enveloped the greenhouse, their bodies gave out and they both lay languidly in the dirt, gazing up into the darkness.

After the pounding of their hearts subsided August sat up abruptly.

"What's the matter?"

"It's all gone wrong, Melissa. We have to go. Tonight. We have to stop Ivanov."

"Go? Where? I don't understand."

"To Silverton. We have to stop them before it's too late."

"I don't think I …"

"You must come. I need your help. And if you stay…"

".. they'll come for me, right? And if I go?"

"They'll come for both of us."

"So let them." Then, from memory, she recited her favorite line of Goethe's poem: "*Many ribbed and toothed, on a surface juicy and swelling, free and unending the shoot seems in fullness to be. Lovingly now the beauteous pairs are standing together, gathered in countless array, there where the altar is raised.*"

THE END
(To be continued)

PART TWO
TWO TALES OF DESIRE

Bar Game

The lights of the restaurant are just dim enough to obscure my imperfections, but still bright enough to see the lovely food. Unobtrusive music fills the room, mingling with the sounds of silverware clinking against plates and the gentle laughter of diners. This eatery is one of those places that costs way too much, but every once in a while you spend half your paycheck to come here because the food is so damned good.

My lover, Eliza, and I have made it a tradition to eat here on our anniversary, and this year, our fifth, Eliza has a special treat in store for me. The evening starts with playful flirting over bitter, icy Campari cocktails. We linger over a seared tuna appetizer, her bare foot rubbing my calves. Then, as we wait for the main course and work on a bottle of 1982 Montrachet as luscious and round as Eliza's ass, with a finish as smooth as her inner thighs, I choose my anniversary gift.

"I want her," I say, pointing to the waitress, a lithe thing with curvy hips, full lips, black hair, and icy blue eyes. Eliza just laughs: "That was my pick, too." She moves across the table and sits right next to me, and begins slowly, verbally unwrapping the present: "Her name is Juliette. She is French. You impress her with your knowledge of food. She's taken with my passion for Paris. Enough so that she agrees to come out for a drink with us after dinner. One glass of Bordeaux later, and her hand is resting on your knee, while yours lingers on her back. One more glass, and she's ready to come home with us."

We call this the bar game. My lover — Eliza hates it when I call her that — and I play it when we are out, just the two of us, at bars or restaurants or sometimes even concerts or plays. After our first drink is finished, and the second sits on the table, cool condensation on its side, Eliza sidles up beside me in the booth and we survey the room. We each pick at least one person – or a couple -- whom we'd like to take home with us. Then, as we discretely touch one another under the table, we take turns verbally unravelling how we plan to approach our prey, what we'll say to them to seduce them into joining us, and what we'll do with them once we get them home.

We never do get them home; never even try. That's not the point of the game. The point, I suppose, is to live out our fantasies and bring one another to excruciating heights of pleasure while sitting in a public establishment. Eliza usually comes out on top (both literally, as soon as we get in the car, and figuratively) thanks to her deft touch, her master storytelling ability and her intimate knowledge of my erogenous zones.

Eliza continues her tale of slow seduction: "On the couch in our apartment, you run your fingers lightly along Juliette's collarbone, barely brushing the soft hairs on the back of her neck. She and I tentatively kiss, our lips touching just enough to send currents of electricity down to our thighs. Our clothes all come off so naturally and slowly that it is almost imperceptible: Your shirt hangs open to reveal your muscular, hairy stomach; my dress is pulled up to my waist; Juliette's white blouse is open, her nipples trying to edge their way through the thin material of her bra. Our hands are everywhere at once, fumbling gracefully over trembling skin, finding hard and soft, smooth and wet."

Back in the reality of the restaurant, Eliza's hand presses up against my hardness through my pants while I try to look as though we are merely chatting about classical music, or a painting we saw, or the day's news, perhaps with a little more than the usual enthusiasm. I doubt I'm fooling anyone. Eliza doesn't miss a beat in her story: "We find ourselves naked, on the floor, our three bodies intertwined. Your eyes are hungry, darting from me to her, wondering which morsel you'll devour next: My achingly wet pussy, or her scrunched up, dark little nipples. We are in a frenzy without focus. Your tongue is in my ass, then it's in Juliette's mouth. My lips are on her nipples, and then wrapped around your cock. We are all pleasurably lost in this universe of flesh."

By the time we finish our main course – lobster in a saffron-butter broth -- Eliza has unzipped my fly and pulled my penis from my pants so that the linen tablecloth brushes against it lightly. Just as the waitress comes to take our lobster plates away, Eliza very indelicately dips her hand into the butter broth, coating her palm with the warm, slick substance. She then reaches back under the table, and slathers my sex with the butter as she takes me gently in her fingers. She slowly strokes me with her thumb as she reaches the climax of her story about the waitress.

"But you can't stand it any more and lift me up on the couch, spread my thighs apart, and go at me with your tongue. Juliette focuses on my breasts, caressing, licking, and sucking them, biting down on my nipples as I come. When you come up for air, your face is covered with my juice and there's an almost mad look of hunger in your eyes," Eliza whispers in my ear as I feed her a stinky chunk of gooey Camembert from our just-arrived cheese plate. "Juliette's hungry, too. Now, I take control, lay her on her side and tell you to get behind her. I reach down and guide you to her, and watch as your sex slips into her warmth. She shudders a bit as you start fucking her from behind, your hands cupping her breasts roughly. As you rhythmically slide into her, and relish the feeling of her soft ass against your belly, my tongue makes its way from her neck to her dark, erect nipples. I kiss her soft belly and then take her waiting clitoris in between my lips and suck deliciously, my tongue flicking in triple-time rhythm to yours. You speed up, her moans increase, and she thrusts her hips – backward towards your cock, forward toward my tongue, until ..."

At exactly that moment, the waitress walks up and announces that the ginger crème brulee is "to die for tonight." Eliza orders for both of us, which is a good thing because she's still working my pleasure spot with her thumb, her rhythm speeding up as she ever so lightly increases the pressure. To both my horror and delight, the waitress lingers, asking if we'd like coffee. I feel my eyes closing involuntarily, my mouth opening but saying nothing, and an orgasm rippling through my body. Eliza expertly catches my come in her hand, and never once loses her composure.

"Coffee would be lovely," I croak, trying not to visibly shudder. "With cream, please."

I have my moments of triumph in the game, too. One chilly, December night, Eliza and I are driving back from a week down on the Gulf of Mexico, returning to life, jobs, routine. On Albuquerque's edge we spy a honky-tonk bar connected to a hotel and decide to stop for one more gulp of uninhibited freedom. It is hot and crowded inside, the light dim, the music loud, and the dance floor hopping. By the time we move from salty-sour margaritas to just plain tequila shots, Eliza's eyes have begun drifting to one particular cowboy's ass in a worn and faded pair of Wranglers.

"That's who I wanna take home tonight," she says as we two-step to a George Strait tune, our backs sweaty from the activity, our necks covered with enough salt to serve as preludes to tequila shots. As we twirl around the dance floor, I steal glimpses of him: He has a square jaw, dark skin and hair, and a smooth shave. He is lean, but muscular. I guess that he has calloused hands, and that his name is Jack.

"You're visiting a huge ranch in Eastern New Mexico for a story you're writing," I whisper into her ear, holding her close on the dance floor. Eliza likes a bit of scene-setting when we play the game – literary foreplay, if you will. "The ranch is owned by some mega-celebrity who's not around, so Jack, the ranch foreman, is showing you around. He's a smart guy, turns out. He knows all about range management, and actually compares a field of thigh-deep grass, waving in the wind, to a passage in a Tolstoy novel."

As that particular song dies out, we amble slowly back to our booth in the corner. The darkness and noise make us feel invisible, and allows me more leeway to accentuate the words of my story with more immediate sensations. It doesn't hurt at all that Eliza is wearing a short skirt, and no underwear. Starting at her knee, I move my hand very slowly up her thigh as I described her fictional day with Jack.

"Eventually, the day leads to evening, with shadows stretched long across the fields of grass. And your professional inquisitiveness has turned to a more personal curiosity. As you're about to regretfully bid adieu, Jack invites you on a ride and a picnic dinner down yonder. You hesitate, then accept. He pulls you up on the back of his horse, tells you to hang on tight, and the two of you gallop off towards a gathering of tall cottonwood trees at the edge of a little mesa, each gallop providing a little shot of stimulation between your thighs.

"You sit underneath the tree in grass that you almost can't see over. He pours you wine, cracks open some oysters on the half shell that had been sitting on ice. They slide down your throat cool and easy. He talks about the time he lived in Paris, in pursuit of the shy dancer who broke his heart."

We get up and dance again. I'm holding Eliza close, pressing my hardness against her, my hand underneath her shirt, gently caressing the small of her back.

"He pushes you back into the grass and kisses you. You look beyond his face, to the cottonwood leaves fluttering in the breeze against the lavender sky of dusk. His lips are strangely soft and warm, almost womanly, in contrast to his muscular body. You feel your own hips rise involuntarily to meet the bulge in his pants, and he takes the opportunity to slip off your damp underwear and to push your skirt up to your waist."

My story is working, and Eliza's dancing becomes clumsy with lust. I take her back to the booth and shamelessly put my hands on her, hoping no one notices the groping couple in the corner. My hand reached her coarse pubic hairs, and my finger slides easily inside of her. Another finds her clitoris, engorged to a bud of pleasure as big as the end of my thumb. I slowly circle it with one finger, while another explores inside. As difficult as it is to keep my cool, I keep telling the story: "As he kisses your mouth and nibbles on your neck, you reach down and undo his pants. His cock almost jumps out, and as you hold on to it, you are astounded by its girth, its hardness, and the heat that emanates from it. You want it inside of you, but he just keeps nibbling on your neck."

By this time, I have managed to contort my right hand into a yogi-like position, with my thumb making circles around and over her clitoris, and two fingers inside her, tickling the nerve endings at the top of her vagina. My left hand is wrapped around her shoulder, underneath her shirt, cupping the weight of her breast and squeezing her nipple between my fingers. She leans back, one of her legs propped up on the table, her eyes closed. If anyone looks towards our table, they will either figure out what is going on, or think that my lover has entered a tequila-induced coma and I am trying to resuscitate her with an unorthodoxed medical maneuver.

I continue the story: "You finally whisper, almost shout, in his ear, 'Quit fucking around and just fuck me.' His look is one of a deer on the side of the road after being hit by a car, but that is replaced by the look of a mountain lion about to pounce. He hardly pauses as he plunges into you, his girth filling you up so that you can feel it all the way up to your nipples."

That's when she comes so hard that, to stifle her scream, she bends over and bites my shoulder, leaving a bruise that will remain for the next week. A group of people standing nearby look at us curiously; I just smile. With a post-coital glow smeared all over her face, Eliza slinks down into the booth, almost laying down. But she sits up to attention, ready to go again, when a waitress, chewing gum, wearing a t-shirt that dangles from her perky breasts and reveals her belly button, approaches. Her eyes linger on mine as I order another round of tequila shots, with limes, no salt necessary. As the waitress – we'll call her Peggy for the story's sake – heads back to the bar, I turn to Eliza.

"It's still an hour to closing time," I say, "and I want her." Eliza smiles and sits back, laying her hand on my thigh. And she begins another story.

Pears and Polaroids

It is the time of year when pears hang heavy from the trees, teasing with their not-quite-ripeness. It is hot and if you are still and watch closely, you can see the pavement melt outside the window of the Artist's little apartment and studio. Telephone wires crisscross the pale blue sky, the sun is still high, and splotches of shade stagger around on the sidewalk.

It is Sunday morning. That's normally when the Artist and I make love. If we miss our Sunday morning rendezvous, maybe we'll make up for it on the Monday or Tuesday after. But that throws off the whole rhythm. That's how I like to think about it: not as if our desire has dried up or become formulaic, but as if we have simply modulated our one-time frantic hunger and found a nice rhythm that we can both jive to. And besides, I know exactly how long a box of condoms will last.

This morning we have not made love and we will not make love because the Artist has one rule, or maybe an exception to the Sunday love-making rule: When she's reaching the creative climax of a piece she's working on, no sex. She thinks it saps her artistic vigor. She's had this rule for as long as I've known her, but in the early days of our relationship, long before the Sunday rule went into effect, back when every morning and every evening was a Sunday, we found interesting ways around it. Back then she would allow me to sit in such a way that I could see her but not the canvas. I masturbated as I watched her paint. Sometimes she'd unbutton her paint-splattered shirt while she worked; sometimes she'd caress herself with one hand, painting with the other, torturing me. Never, however, did she relent.

But that was then, and we've spent many seasons together and now I'm too shy even to ask if I can watch her paint, let alone get myself off while she works. Instead, I sit restlessly in the apartment next to the pear tree. The Artist sits here, too. All that separates us is a small wooden table, an empty green bottle, a Mason jar half full of red wine, and a pear.

From the silence that grows between two people who have said all they have to say to one another, I speak. "What are you working on?"

"Oh," she says, "not much."

I wait

"You know I don't talk about my work. Not before it's done."

"Yeah," I say. "And even then…"

Another pause.

"A pear," she says.

"You're painting a pear?"

"Yeah, and I need to get back to it."

"I get it," I say, wanting to be involved somehow. "You're trying to capture the true form of Pear, with a capital P. The essence. The Archetype. The part of the Pear that endures. Infinite Pear. Forever Pear."

"Or maybe I'm doing exactly the opposite," she says, a hint of irritation in her voice.

"Is this the pear you're painting?" I pick up the fruit on the table, ponder its surprising weight, its freckles, its scars, the tiny bent stem, and the way it manages to be both golden and green all at once. In this moment I desperately want to know how she'll paint it. Will it be a hurried affair — frenzied caresses in the squeaky backseat of an old Pontiac? Or long, languid, maddening in its slowness?

She tries to give me one of those looks, but I avoid it by making eyes at the jar of red wine. Although it flirts a little, it is aware of my desperation and eventually gets up and sidles off with the green bottle. I want to tell her that pears are unremarkable, that there are four types at the local grocery store, that there is even a small pear tree outside the window of my apartment. I say nothing.

I am the Artist's Lover. She hates both terms. She's not an artist, but someone who does art, she says. "So by that logic, we're not lovers, but people who make love," I say. No, no, she says, that word's so pretentious, corny. How about partner, she says, or companion? Those aren't enough, I say, they don't capture what we are, the essence, the Sunday mornings.

I became her lover many years ago in early summer. I was someone else's lover at the time. So the artist crept slowly and surreptitiously into my life. In the beginning we talked. Then we lay in the park and read Shakespeare together. Then I started walking her to her home in a sketchy neighborhood at night. Then she said why don't I just stay at your place tonight, save you the trouble? Then we woke up and she kissed me and kept on kissing me.

For weeks, that's all we did, feeling shy and a little guilty afterward, especially when people saw us together and knew. They could read it in the way we looked at one another, in the slight flush that rose to our cheeks.

Then one day during that short period when the lilacs are in full and immodest bloom, and their scent wakes you up deep in the night, like an irrepressible itch, we kissed, but knew that we would not stop there. We didn't talk about it beforehand. We didn't map out how it would go. It's just that our lips wandered. Our hands explored. Our clothes came off. It was in the afternoon, so I could see her, see the rosy-olive tint of her skin, the way her hip bones jutted softly from the valley beside her belly, her firm breasts, her pink nipples.

I remember both my hunger and my reticence. I wanted to plunge myself inside of her, and I wanted her in me. But I also didn't want to cross that line, which is no different than the one that separates summer from fall. A sharp line. One moment everything is still possible, as in late July walking through a field of thigh-high grass and flowers. The next you are struggling to break free of the clinging memories of adolescence and lost love. The light shifts, ever so subtly, and you notice a hint of yellow in the leaves, a strand of gray among the brown, an ache where there wasn't one before.

But the Artist, back then, was impatient. She wanted none of my gentle caresses, none of my bewildered gaze, none of my languid getting-her-into-the-mood bullshit. She wanted to rush towards that line, cross it, then cross it again. "Condom," she said, grabbing my penis. "Condom. Where?"

I pointed to the little box on the milk crate by the futon on my floor. She tore open the package, rolled it onto my sex, while I clenched my eyes shut, trying desperately not to come in her hands. She opened her legs wide, in the broad daylight, her sex a hothouse flower, beckoning. She pulled me to her, hungrily.

"Not yet, not yet," I said. I wanted to savor the moment, hold the crossing of the line at bay, know her taste. Before she could protest, I buried my face in her sex. She would have none of that.

"Arrrrgh," she shrieked. "That's. Just. Making. Me. Hornier!"

Needless to say, we crossed the line. And even as I clenched my teeth in the agony of orgasm, her hands pulling me into her, I mourned the loss of the moment that preceded it.

In the weeks that followed, the sheets on the futon on my apartment's floor were often damp with our sweat, tangled up in our legs, and wrapped around our bodies. We got confused about whose flesh was whose. Her hair spilled across the pillow like a stain. Her hand, palm open in longing, blooming against the white plaster wall. The only words uttered were those of the meaningless poem I traced with my fingertips in the hallowed cusp beside her hip, and the prayers I moaned on the altar of her thighs.

It was summer when I became the Artist's Lover. The soft, warm breeze and the porchlight caused the leaves on the pear tree to flicker and glow.

I used to stay up late at night, feverishly writing down everything I had seen and felt and experienced. I called myself a writer. I wanted to think of myself as an artist. But the more words I wrote down, the less weight they seemed to have. Words, I found, were unable to capture light, sliding across a hayfield after June rain. They can't communicate the surprising pull of the pear as it tugs free from the branch in late September, or the fruit's subtle aroma just before teeth penetrate flesh, or the gravity pulling on a lover's breast cupped in one's palm. They don't have the power to keep the line separating summer from fall at bay.

Words are no match for the Artist's pictures of the pear. And to-day, as I sit across the table from her, the Artist has no more use for words than she did for my mouth on her sex on the afternoon that I became her lover.

So I have decided to embark on a journey to find a new art.

My search begins at the Flea Market. I cannot afford a new art straight from the store, so I will settle for one that has been discarded. I pack up my old art in a tattered cardboard box and take it with me, hoping to make some sort of trade or, if that doesn't work, ditch the box behind one of the booths in such a way that it can't follow me home.

It's dusty at the market and I walk past the African guys selling amber beads, and the old man selling stolen tools, and the Mexican guys with their Madonna and Menudo cassette tapes who ogle the rich white ladies as they walk past. As I try to determine if an old eight-track cassette deck could somehow create art, something catch-es my eye on a dirty old card table with a broken leg. There, beside a black and white TV, sits an old Polaroid camera. I pick it up and turn it around in my hands, appreciating its plastic curves and its plastic weight.

"How much?" I ask the guy behind the table. He wears a Metalli-ca t-shirt and mirrored pilot glasses and has dirty blonde hair, short on the sides, long on top and in back. His teeth are streaked with yel-low and a little crooked, just as an artist's should be.

He removes his glasses and squints at me, looking deep into my eyes. It scares me a bit at first, but then I realize he is just sizing me up, trying to decide if I am worthy of his discarded art-machine. "Three dollars," he finally says.

"Does it work?" I ask. But when I look through the smudged little viewfinder up at the sky, my question is answered. For there, in the tiny window, I see the little trailer where he lives. It sits crookedly on cinder blocks at the far edge of a long row of other trailers where the city's sprawl meets up with the desert. A woman drives up in an old Ford Fiesta, one window spiderwebbed with cracks, a cloud of dust following her. She shuts down the car, listens to the engine tick for a minute, then pulls herself out into the hot air. She wears tight jeans and a long-sleeved white shirt, her work uniform. She walks into the stagnant air of the trailer. Her boyfriend, the man at the Flea Market, waits anxiously.

"Take off your clothes," he says.

"Aww, Frank. Not now, I'm tired," she replies. "Maybe after I have a drink and watch my show."

"No, no, not that," he says. "Look what I got. A Polaroid. I just want to take a picture of you."

She smiles wearily, sighs resignedly. She turns away from him and, facing the brown paneling, pulls off her shirt, then slips off the jeans. She starts to slide off her underwear, noticing that the elastic has lost its power, grown tired. She'd need to make a trip to Target for a new pair.

"Wait, wait," the man says, holding up his hands in a square shape and looking at her through it, like the film directors on TV. "Leave them on."

She flops down on the couch and reaches for a cigarette, but then sees the disappointment in his eyes, so instead lies down in what she hopes is a flattering way, propping herself up on one elbow, holding the other arm behind her head. When the man with the Polaroid looks through the viewfinder, he sees something that he had never seen before. He moves closer to her, then back, trying to find the right composition. He's a perfectionist. Finally he pushes the button, the flash splashes the room with sharp light, the motor whirs loudly, and the little rectangle of thick and shiny paper emerges from the slot. He sits down on the couch next to her, more transfixed by the image slowly coming into view than by the woman sitting almost naked next to him. As she looks at the picture and the pale blue light that seems to infuse it, she realizes, for the first time in her life, that she is beautiful, bruises and all.

"Do you want the camera, or what?" he asks with threat in his voice, ripping me out of my reverie. I dig into my pocket and pull out four crumpled up dollar bills and toss them on the table, too embarrassed to wait around for the change. Before walking away, I stash the box containing my art underneath his rickety old card table.

After the Artist and I had crossed the line from the first summer of our relationship into the first autumn, she became very specific about what she wanted and when. Her preferred mode of lovemaking involved me sitting on the bed, my back against the wall, while she straddled me. It put her into control, allowed her to thrust me deep inside or just hold me barely within her lips. It allowed her to grind her clitoris into my pubic bone, and it allowed her to stop altogether if she sensed my orgasm coming too quickly. It allowed her to drive me mad.

When she was about to come, the skin on her neck and chest bloomed with pink flowers, her movements became frenzied, she tossed her head back, and she muttered, "now-now-now-now-now," which was the signal for me to squeeze her breasts together and to bite her nipple and to finally let myself go — as if I could control it anyway.

As autumn became winter, I made her slow down a little. She grudgingly began allowing me to go down on her, at first merely as prelude, but later as an end in itself. Then when she was sleepy or in a languid mood, she started asking for it, pleading with me to take my time, to be gentle with my tongue. She'd lay back and groan as I sucked on her labia, as they slid between my lips and teeth like an oyster, fresh from the shell. I flicked my tongue across the very tip of her clitoris, so lightly that it was almost like she was being caressed by the wind.

While giving me a blow job once, as I writhed around on the bed uncontrollably, whimpering with pleasure, she stopped abruptly, licked her lips, and stated, in a stern voice: "I'm glad you seem to be enjoying this, but I honestly don't care. I'm doing it because it gives *me* pleasure." When my face is buried in her sex, slathered with her juices, her thighs clamping down on the side of my head, her breaths turning to gasps, her clitoris all swollen between my teeth, I have the exact same thought. I'm not sure if that makes me a better person, or a worse one.

I hurry home from the Flea Market, stopping at the grocery store to buy some film and the ripest pear I can find and a cheap bottle of wine. When I get to my apartment, it's already dusk. Music and the sounds of the night blend in the warm air. Venus lingers in the purple-glass sky in the west. Do you remember those nights when you were young and smooshed up in the booth at Dennys next to the person you just met that night and they are running their fingers slowly up and down your thigh under the table almost absentmindedly and you think maybe something will happen but you really don't care because you want the moment to last forever, the cloying sweetness of the hot chocolate, the surly waitress, their touch, possibility? Do you remember?

That's precisely how Venus looks tonight as it slides slowly toward the horizon.

I set the pear down on the windowsill, load the camera with film, and make a picture of the pear. I watch as the photo transforms from a ghost to an image. It is an old family snapshot, circa 1976, colors both muted and gaudy, saturated and faded: brown sweater, mustard yellow slacks, washed-out turquoise sky, dad's bushy mustache and sideburns. Lipstick too bright, smiles too big, that strange seventies dreaminess. I snap another, and recoil a bit when the image gels. This time the pear is a crime scene, washed out by a too-enthusiastic flash: The body in a dumpster behind an all-night diner on a busy street in Los Angeles, dress all crumpled up around thighs. They never found the killer, never even tried.

I try to call the Artist so I can show her the pictures of the pear, but she never answers. So I drink too much red wine and lay down on the futon on the floor, anxiety bearing down on me. It is that time of year, after all. Every year, sometimes in late August, sometimes in early September, when I sense the approach of that moment when the seasons shift, I become anxious, restless. I become consumed with the belief that if I move southward quickly enough I can stay ahead of the line, I can dodge the malaise it carries with it. It's not because I'm afraid of what's on the other side of the line — dead leaves, cold nights, tempered lust, a touch of ennui — but because I'm afraid of what I'll lose by crossing it.

When I awake the first thing I see is the pear tree outside my window. The camera sits on my cluttered desk, the photos of the pear sitting next to it. And, much to my dismay, my old art lies patiently on the floor. It's still packed up in the box, but it's there, nonetheless, staring at me with desperation in its eyes. Perhaps if I just leave it will be gone when I come back. Or maybe I should make it breakfast, tell it I had fun but I'm not really interested in a relationship. The phone rings. It's the Artist. She has finished her paintings. It is Sunday morning.

I don't open the box. Instead I pick up the photos, put them into my pocket, and walk to her apartment. I open the door without knocking and she is there, smiling in a way that I haven't seen in a long time. She is not painting and the canvases that once leaned against the wall are gone.

"Where are your paintings?" I ask, frozen in the doorway.

"I sold them," she replies.

"Oh," I respond, and she guides me gently to her bed.

On that Sunday morning we make love following variation number one: light caresses, leading to heavy caresses, leading to my lips and tongue following the curves of her flesh. Cunnilingus until she reaches orgasm. Intercourse, in the missionary position, until I do the same. Sometimes we fuck before I go down on her. Sometimes she's on top. Sometimes I take her from behind, her luscious ass rubbing softly up against my hairy belly. Sometimes I burst like a too-ripe tomato in her hand. But generally we follow a set pattern, with variations.

Don't misunderstand. The fervor of our lovemaking has not ebbed, even after we've crossed the seasonal line so many times together. When we are in the throes of it, I am a rat, being digested by a snake. My bones dissolve beneath my skin. Her cries come from somewhere down below. I forget whose body parts belong to whom. Her pelvis gyrates frenetically. My mental movie screen explodes with color. Spasms ripple through her vagina when she comes.

Nor has my hunger for her diminished with old age. On days that aren't Sunday, thoughts of her on Sunday morning still sidle into my head unexpectedly, and I get so aroused that I cannot accomplish anything else until I come. As I stroke myself at my little writing desk I summon other fantasies that don't involve her — former lovers, strangers, kinky sex acts, men, women — but in the end, as my caresses become fervent, she always butts her way back in, and it's to visions of her that semen bursts onto my belly, that shudders reverberate up my spine.

"Let's go get something to eat," she says, "it's on me."

All that separates us is a table, some dirty plates, a glass with orange juice pulp on its side, and the pear, which has grown ripe and almost rotten with waiting. A vision of the leafless pear tree floods my mind. It is stark and almost black against the cold sky, its branches holding snow as softly as someone holds a sadness that will never end. The Artist and I don't have a lot to say. The pear is absolutely silent. I don't mind. The words will come when they're ready. But she is fidgeting, looking restlessly toward the window. Searching.

"I think we crossed the line again," I say, motioning toward the shadows on the sidewalk outside. "Before you know it, winter will be here."

One summer when I was younger, back before I met the Artist, back when I was perched on the border between the past and the future, my friends and I went to a park down by the river late one evening, the cool grass prickly against bare feet. It was an unremarkable park, but had the best swing set around. We all got on those swings, and pumped until we were going so high that there was slack in the chain at the apex of each cycle, a moment of freefall before the jerk of the chain catching. Cool air rose off the river and blew against my face and tears caught in the corner of my eye, and for a little moment, time was nothing, the line disappeared, autumn would never arrive. I heard the pfffft sound fro the automated sprinklers, a loud hiss, but before I could register what it meant, the icy water collided with my face, my legs, my chest, tearing the breath from me, exhilarating. Alive.

Sometimes when the Artist and I are at a party, mingling, I will look up, and through the blur of the crowd I will see her, vibrant, her cheeks blushed with the excitement of conversation, her long hair falling over her shoulders, her big lips accentuating her big teeth, and it sends a jolt through me that feels exactly like the spray of that sprinkler on those warm summer nights so long ago.

I pick up the pear and take a bite. She only smiles.

About the Author

Malcolm Brautigan first emerged into the public consciousness by way of *Sultan's Secret*, a serialized novel by Jonathan P. Thompson that appeared on the back page of *The Silverton Mountain Journal* beginning in 2000. Brautigan was also the main character in *White Noise* and the *Atomic Rooster*. He was the editor of the *Dandelion Times* in Silverton, Colorado, before becoming the environment and science reporter for the *Tucson Tribune*. In 2015 he founded *Alt-News*, and ran it until his conscience managed a hostile takeover and disbanded the operation, as detailed in the forthcoming novel, *Behind the Slickrock Curtain*. Now he is lead chocolate chip cookie baker for Better than Keks, a business that peddles baked goods outside Berlin nightclubs.

Malcolm Brautigan is fictional and a figment of Jonathan P. Thompson's imagination. Any resemblance to an actual person, living or dead, is purely coincidental.